Four-ever Single

Samantha Baca

Just One Time

Second Chances

Third Time's The Charm

Four-ever Single

Fifth Wheel

Cover Design: Richard Baca
Image(s): DepositPhotos

Contents

Contents

One

Jones

"Should we call the fire department?"

I sighed heavily, letting my shoulders fall as I stared at the fire in the oven. I shook my head.

"Nope. I am the fire department."

"Oh." She rubbed her lips together to keep from saying anything else. I reached into the cabinet and pulled out the fire extinguisher as she moved out of the way.

"Since you seem to have this covered, I guess I'll just…"

I didn't bother to turn around to say goodbye, given the door slammed closed before I could. I shook my head, disappointed in myself, as I put the fire out and opened the doors to let the brisk evening breeze in. It was still a little chilly for the beginning of May, but it matched my mood as I thought about how depressing it was that this date hadn't even made it to dinner before it ended. Sure, it was my fault for not taking the cardboard out from beneath the frozen pizza before cooking it, but still.

It was seven o'clock on a Friday night, and I had the next two days off before I started another 48 hours on. I knew most of the guys at the firehouse would have plans tonight since most were married or dating someone, so I didn't want to bother them. But I also couldn't stay in the house and be left alone with my thoughts. I grabbed my keys, locked the door, and headed out.

The Tipsy Taquito was always busy, but it seemed everyone in Beaumont Creek was here tonight. I placed my order and then grabbed a spot at one of the high-top tables in the back. I didn't love eating alone, but it was better to sit and people-watch than to sit at home and obsess over my failed dating life. *Four-ever Single* was what they would someday write on my tombstone when I succumbed to a burnt food-related death.

Music played loudly over the speakers as the college kids danced and threw back shots. A couple snuggled together in the corner booth beside me, making out like teenagers and reminding me that I was never going to be one of those people. Unlucky in life and even more so in love. That had always been me, and no matter how hard I tried, it would stay that way.

"Hey, what are you doing here?" Capshaw said, pulling out the chair beside me and taking a seat.

"Just grabbing some dinner." I shrugged nonchalantly, hoping my personal life was so boring that he wouldn't remember the date I had tonight.

"What happened? Why aren't you on your date?"

"I burned dinner," I answered quietly, looking away. "I should have taken your advice and gone to Surf 'N Shack instead."

"What did you make?" He leaned back in the chair and folded his arms over his chest.

"Frozen pizza."

He closed his eyes and let his head drop forward.

"I know, I know. Leave it to me to forget to take the cardboard out again," I said with a heavy sigh, already knowing where his thoughts were going. We'd been friends long enough for him to know how terrible of a cook I was. Not only that, but we were also in the same platoon, so he'd been there since I started as a rookie and earned my reputation in the firehouse.

"Did she…"

"Leave right away? Yeah. Before I could get the fire out, she was gone."

"Shit, I'm sorry, man." He sighed heavily and gave me a soft smile.

"It's alright. It's not like the first few dates had gone all that well, to begin with. I'm honestly surprised she agreed to another."

We sat there quietly watching the people around us for a few minutes.

"What are you doing here?" I asked. "I thought you and Kensy had plans?"

"We did, but they changed when Lia insisted the girls come out for a girl's night. Apparently, some guy she had been dating dumped her, and now they were all going to help her drown her sorrows tonight. I was planning to drop Kensy off and come back for the three of them later, but then I spotted you and decided to stay."

"So, you took pity and came to sit with the loser in the corner?"

"You're not a loser, Jones. Don't you let me catch you thinking that way about yourself again. So, you had a shitty date. We've all been there. Shake it off and move on to the next."

A waitress dropped off my food before heading to another table, noting Capshaw's number still sitting on the table.

"You say that like there's a long line of prospects waiting for me."

"There might not be a long line, but the right girl is out there."

He leaned back as his plate of food was delivered, but I was too distracted to hear what he was saying when I spotted Bella across the room dancing. She wasn't just the most beautiful girl I had ever seen, but she was Capshaw's sister's best friend, and I had recently spent a lot of time with her as I helped Capshaw get them moved into their new house. Just being in her presence was enough to pull me in and captivate me. I had slowly been falling for her ever since, reminding myself that someone like Bella would never go for a guy like me.

But that didn't stop me from watching as her body moved in perfect rhythm with the beat, her long, curly hair swaying just above her hips, entrancing me. I could look, but I would never be lucky enough to touch.

"So what do you think?" Capshaw asked, popping a chip into his mouth.

I pulled my attention away from Bella, having no idea what he just asked.

"About what?" I asked cautiously, hoping he hadn't caught me checking her out.

He shook his head, and a smirk crossed his face as he looked past me to where the girls were dancing. Kensy looked around until she spotted us and waved, her eyes lighting up when they landed on mine. She turned to Bella and pulled her in, but they both had their backs to us, so I couldn't see what she was saying. Very discreetly, Bella looked over her shoulder at us and then turned away, embarrassed that she got caught.

"She's single," Capshaw said, dipping his chip into the cup of guacamole on his plate.

"Who is?" I asked, wiping my mouth with a napkin, brows pulled together in confusion. My heart started racing because I already knew what he was going to say.

"Bella."

I opened my mouth to say something along the lines of how I wasn't interested in her but shut it when I saw his smug grin growing bigger, confirming he already knew.

"I'm not her type," I said instead, lowering my eyes to my plate. It was easier to remind myself that I was out of her league than it was to entertain the thoughts of ever having a girl like Bella.

"I wouldn't be so sure of that," he said quietly as we caught her looking in our direction. I looked away and focused on my food so my heart didn't get confused and start getting my hopes up.

An hour passed with us bullshitting and talking about stuff at the firehouse. I was thankful for the company, and it was like the universe had taken pity on me by keeping me from spending the night alone in my apartment.

I got up and headed down the narrow hallway to the bathrooms. I squeezed against the wall to let a couple of girls pass since there wasn't enough room for all of us with their arms linked together. They appeared to be drunk but happy as they stumbled past me back to the dance area. I was about to go into the men's restroom when I spotted Bella coming out of the women's restroom. A few guys were lingering in the hallway, one nudging the other and nodding in her direction.

I couldn't hear what was being said, but I felt the fire pulse through my veins as I watched the taller one snake his arm around her waist and try to whisper something in her ear. She immediately frowned and tried to push him off her, but he pulled her tighter against him.

"Get off her," I growled, taking a few steps toward them and shoving his chest until she was free from his grasp.

His eyebrows pinched together as he looked down at me, fury raging behind his eyes.

"Who are you? Her little bodyguard?" he asked mockingly.

I grabbed her hand and pulled her behind me, ignoring the shivers that ran through me as she grabbed tightly to the back of my shirt. Now wasn't the time to think about the electrical current I felt from touching her.

"She's not interested. Back the fuck off."

"Or what? You going to make me?"

He raised his chin and stared at me, his fists clenched at his sides. I had no problem laying him out, but I was more worried about Bella being too close. I couldn't take both guys at the same time and keep an eye on her.

"Walk away," I said sharply, pulling my shoulders back and leveling him with a look. "Save the cleaning crew from having to mop your blood off the floors after I get done smashing your face in."

Something that looked a lot like fear flickered in his eyes as I tilted my head and stared at him. My jaw tightened as I struggled to keep myself calm. His friend stepped beside him, making his presence known, but I ignored him and the stupid remarks he was making about Bella.

I worked my jaw back and forth, hoping that Bella would be smart enough to run away if things took a turn. I wasn't worried about taking on these two douchebags, but I couldn't stand the thought of her getting hurt in the process.

"I'm not going to tell you again," I warned. "Leave before I knock your ass out."

Suddenly, their eyes shifted to behind me, and their features changed. I didn't have to look back to know Capshaw was standing there watching us.

"Whatever," he muttered, nodding for his friend to follow him. They walked past, each shoulder checking me on the way. Once they were out of sight, I turned toward Bella and studied her.

"Are you okay?" I asked, trying to keep from reaching out and touching her.

"Yeah. Thank you. I'm sorry about that."

"You have nothing to apologize for. No is a complete sentence, and I have no problem making sure they understand it."

She smiled and tucked a strand of curly hair behind her ear.

I looked past her to see Capshaw standing at the end of the hallway, arms folded over his chest, with Lia and Kensy standing beside him.

"Looks like it's time to go," I said, placing my hand on her lower back and guiding her out.

"Everything okay?" Capshaw asked once we reached them.

"Yeah."

He nodded and wrapped his arm around Kensy's waist before leading his sister, Lia, toward the door. The crowd had grown, making it nearly impossible to move through the bodies on the makeshift dance floor.

"Oh my God! You're the firefighters from the calendar!" A drunk girl shrieked, grabbing her friend's arm and spinning her to face us. "Will you sign my bra?" she asked Capshaw with a huge grin, not noticing his arm around Kensy. Or more so, not caring.

She started lifting her shirt at the same time Lia raised her fist before Capshaw stopped her.

"Not tonight, Lia. You're never going to make it through med school if you get arrested for getting into a fight," he warned loudly, pushing her through the crowd and out the door. The loud music faded once we were outside, stepping into the crisp evening air.

"Don't you get tired of women throwing themselves at you guys because of some stupid calendar?" Lia asked, tripping over her own feet as she stumbled beside Capshaw. He reached out and grabbed her elbow to steady her without letting go of his hold on Kensy.

"It's not a stupid calendar, Lia. It was for charity and made a lot of money that they needed," Capshaw corrected.

"Yeah, a lot of money from women who take it home and mastur—"

"For the love of God, don't finish that sentence," he muttered, steering her toward his truck as she hiccupped loudly.

"I'll take Lia and Kensy in my truck," Capshaw said, looking at me. "Can you drive Bella?"

"Why can't we all go in your truck?" Lia asked, her words slightly slurred.

"There's not enough room."

Capshaw kept his eyes on me while Kensy grinned, knowing what her fiancé was up to. Lia frowned, not understanding it.

"I don't mind getting a ride with Jones if he doesn't mind taking me," Bella said softly by my side.

"I don't mind at all."

"Great. It's settled. Let's get these girls home before they throw up in my truck," Capshaw said, eyeing his sister.

Two
Bella

"Thank you for driving me home," I said, tugging my skirt down. It wasn't super short, but I didn't want to come across as *that kind of girl* to Jones. Not that he'd even allowed himself to glance in my direction. From the moment he helped me into the truck, he'd gone rigid, gripping the steering wheel so tight that his knuckles turned white. A guy like Jones likely wanted a *nice* girl he could take home to meet his parents, not one who made money from people ogling her body.

"Not a problem," he replied, looking out his window as we stopped at a red light.

"And thank you for what you did back there. With those guys…" I twirled a strand of hair around my finger, the curl bouncing back tighter than before. He made me nervous but in a good way.

"I didn't do much."

"You kept me from being put in a position I didn't want to be in. That means a lot."

I paused and thought carefully about my next words.

"Ever since word has gotten out about my recent assignment with Dark Vibes, I've gotten some *unwanted* attention from it. I knew it was a whole different game doing lingerie modeling, but I honestly didn't expect the news to spread through town the way it did. The men think I'm some walking wet dream while the women are lighting their torches. I get that Dark Vibes is a sex toy company, but it's not like I'm doing live videos showing how to use them. Their company is very progressive and focused on women's empowerment."

"I've found that nothing stays secret in a small town for long," he offered quietly. "I was definitely surprised by that when I moved here, with all the unwanted attention I've gotten. You're beautiful inside and out, Bella. Don't let what others think of you get to you. They have bigger issues if they have time to sit around and judge you for being a model."

"You seem to be getting quite a bit of attention from the calendar. I've seen the women around town checking you out," I teased, hoping he recognized the playful tone in my voice.

"It's the other guys in it that have the women in town drooling. I'm just the one who everyone talks about or looks at when something catches fire."

My heart sank with the sadness in his voice.

"I don't think that about you," I said, gently touching his arm.

He looked down at it but didn't pull away like I expected him to. He also looked completely unsure of what to do, so I pulled back and folded my hands in my lap.

"Thank you," he replied, flipping on his turn signal as he followed Capshaw to my house. Technically, it was mine and Lia's, but she hadn't been around much lately. Between finishing medical school and spending time with the guy she was dating, it was like having the whole place to myself.

He pulled into the driveway and put his truck in park but didn't make any move to get out. It was as if he didn't want this time between us to end any more than I did.

"Um, do you want to come inside and have a cup of coffee?" I offered, wincing when I sounded like some old lady from the cheesy late-night reruns Lia made me watch with her. I looked out the window and rolled my eyes. *Way to go, Bella. Sounding so desperate and needy.*

"You don't have to," I rushed out. "I don't know if coffee this late is even a good idea. I mean, it's not super late or anything, but who wants to be all jacked up on caffeine? I mean, I guess some people because they might have stuff to do. But not me. I mean, it's not that I don't have a life—I totally do. But working out in the morning isn't something that requires a ton of sleep tonight. So you know, if you wanted to—"

"I'd love to come in for a cup of coffee," he said, interrupting me. "But maybe we should consider decaf." He winked playfully, sending a jolt straight to my vagina before getting out of the truck and coming around to help me out.

Capshaw was already unlocking the door while Kensy held Lia up. Lia had been determined to get drunk enough to forget her problems for the night, while Kensy and I had no desire to get wasted. She had plans with her fiancé that she didn't want to miss, and I didn't need to consume extra calories by drinking them right now. I had another photoshoot in a few days and needed to make sure I was at my absolute best for it. Unflattering swelling from the excessive sugar intake Lia was demanding would only be detrimental to me.

We followed them inside, and I kicked my heels off and set them on the rack by the door before hanging my purse on the hook above it. Jones had been to our house with Capshaw a few times, so I wasn't surprised when he kicked off his shoes and set them beside mine.

"I'm going to make some coffee. Anyone want some?" I offered as Lia fought Kensy on going to bed.

"I'll have some," Lia hiccupped, plopping down on the couch as Kensy struggled to get her knee-high boots off of her.

"You need sleep," Kensy said, grunting as she pulled so hard she started to fall back.

Capshaw steadied her before moving her out of the way and tugging his sister's boots off. He picked them up and took them to the rack while Lia tugged at her off-the-shoulder sweater and grumbled about how tight her pants were. She had insisted on getting dressed up tonight, but Kensy and I knew she would be complaining about the tight attire before the night was over. Lia much preferred wearing scrubs and tennis shoes, so it was always a big deal when she decided to attempt heels.

"I'm not tired," Lia objected, swatting her brother and Kensy away. "I just need loose pants and a cup of coffee.

Or maybe another shot so I can forget about that asshole…” She hiccupped again, wiping a tear away.

“Or maybe, some sleep. You’ll feel better in the morning, which is all the more reason to get you into some comfy pajamas and into bed,” Kensy said, giving Lia the look.

I turned on the Keurig, grabbed the spinning carousel with pods, and set it on the counter in front of Jones.

“What would you like?” I asked, ignoring the butterflies in my stomach as his fingers brushed against mine when he reached over to spin it.

“What are you having?”

“Decaf coffee, black. I already drank too many calories tonight,” I said with a soft sigh.

“I’ll do the same.”

“I can make you something else,” I offered. “Lia has some caramel vanilla—”

“Touch my coffee and die,” she called over her shoulder as Kensy guided her to her room.

I laughed, loving that there was never a dull moment with my hot-headed best friend.

“She won’t really kill you,” I said with a grin, feeling nervous when Capshaw came over to the island and pulled out the stool beside Jones.

“She probably will,” he corrected, nudging Jones. “I told you about the time I ate her Baby Ruth.”

"You're lucky you didn't lose a limb," I said, feeling Jones' eyes on me. "She didn't stop talking about that for months. It was so exhausting; I was ready to come murder you myself over it."

"How did you finally get her to stop?" Jones asked.

"I bought her a new one and pretended that Capshaw had felt bad and bought it for her." I shrugged.

"Did she ever find out?"

"Nope," I said, letting the *p* pop. "And if you tell her, I will come for you." I narrowed my eyes at Capshaw, making my warning clear.

"What are you coming for my fiancé for now?" Kensy asked, wrapping her arms around Capshaw's neck as he pulled her into his arms.

"Just giving him a *friendly warning* about him not saying a word about the replacement Baby Ruth."

Kensy's eyes widened, and she shook her head.

"Yeah, I have to agree with Bella. If you say anything, I'll withhold sex for two months." She looked down at him and pinned him with a look. "We will make you as miserable as she made us."

"I think withholding sex is going to hurt you as much as it hurts me," he teased playfully. I imagined he had meant for only her to hear it, but since I couldn't *unhear* it, I busied myself with popping a K-cup into the machine and brewing Jones' coffee.

"Is she in bed?" Capshaw asked, tickling Kensy's sides.

"Yeah. She fought me, but once her head hit the pillow, she was out," Kensy said.

"Did her head hit the pillow, or did you hit her in the head with the pillow until you knocked her out?" I teased, raising an eyebrow.

"Does it matter? She's out." She shrugged and tried to fight her grin.

"Nope. But if she gets me up to eat cookie dough in the middle of the night, I'm calling you."

Kensy scrunched her face, grimacing.

"Remind me to put my phone on *Do Not Disturb*," she teased.

I placed my hands on my hips and glared at her.

"You know I can't eat that stuff, Kens. How about taking one for the team?" I batted my eyes playfully at her. I was just goading her, but it was what we did best now that we spent so much time together with her being my photographer. "Unless you plan to edit out all of the new bulges and rolls I'm going to get from trying to be a good friend…" I pulled my mouth to the side and leaned against the counter.

"I'll take one for the team," Jones said, clearing his throat. "I don't mind eating cookies in the middle of the night."

My cheeks burned with embarrassment as I struggled *not* to take what he said the wrong way. *Wishful thinking, Bella. Wishful thinking.*

18

Three
Jones

I don't mind eating cookies in the middle of the night?!

I stifled my groan before it could come out, but hated how I sounded like such a dumbass. Capshaw turned his head and chuckled, trying to hide it behind a cough. I lowered my head but caught a glimpse of the blush on Bella's cheeks.

"Well, it's getting late. We better get going," Capshaw said, pushing his stool out and standing. "Call us *only* if it's an emergency." He raised his eyebrows at Bella, driving his point across.

"*Everything* with your sister is an emergency," she teased. "But go, we'll be fine. She's probably passed out for the night anyway. I'll set some water and Tylenol out for her before I go to the gym in the morning."

Bella walked them out and then locked the door, leaving me standing awkwardly in the kitchen, unsure if I should go too.

"Do you want to watch a movie?" she asked, grabbing both cups of coffee from the counter and smiling as she walked into the living room, waiting for me to follow her.

"Sure," I replied with uncertainty. "I don't want to impose, so feel free to kick me out whenever you want to."

"You're not imposing, silly. I asked you to come in and have a cup of coffee. Trust me, I'm not ready for bed yet, and it would be nice to have some company."

She handed me my cup and then curled up in the corner of the couch, smiling as she waited for me to sit next to her. I steadied my hands to keep from spilling the hot liquid all over myself as I sat an appropriate distance next to her. If I sat too close, it would likely come off as me wanting to get handsy with her, whereas if I sat too far away, it would appear that I was uninterested in her.

She took a sip of her coffee, then set it on a coaster before picking up the remote and turning the TV on. I followed her lead, having a sip without burning my tongue, then placed it on the coffee table.

I watched as she flipped through the channels, neither of us paying any attention to what was on the TV.

"Did you feel the spark?" she asked casually, not looking at me as her gaze stayed locked on the TV.

I furrowed my brow in confusion.

"Earlier, when we touched. Was it just me, or did you feel it too?" she clarified.

"Oh," I said, dumbfounded, clearing my throat. "That."

I turned and studied her face, wondering why she brought it up. She set the remote down and lifted her mug to her lips, watching me intently as she waited for my answer.

"Yeah, I felt it," I admitted, rubbing my lips together.

"Have you felt that with anyone before?"

I shook my head, enjoying the flush of color tinting her olive-toned cheeks.

"Me neither," she admitted. "And I've dated a lot of guys. Well—not *a lot*, but enough that I have plenty of experience with dating, yet I've never had that happen before."

I licked my lips, my whole mouth suddenly going dry.

"So," she said slowly, exhaling a long, deep breath. "What should we do about it?"

I swallowed hard, hoping she didn't notice the way my Adam's apple protruded from it.

"What do you want to do about it?" I asked quietly.

She chewed her lower lip as she set her mug back on the coffee table.

"Well… I don't know about you, but I thought it might be fun to explore it and see what it is."

My eyebrows shot up my forehead in disbelief. Was she really insinuating that she and I should hook up? A beautiful girl like her was interested in fooling around with *me?*

"Ummm…" I hesitated.

"Shit," she muttered quickly, looking away. "I'm sorry. I must have read this wrong. I thought you felt what I felt, and maybe you would be interested in—you know what? Never mind. I'm sorry. I shouldn't have mentioned it. Let's just forget I said anything."

She looked away as she reached for the remote again. Before I could think about it, I reached over and took it from her, tossing it to the rug. Her eyes widened as I grabbed her arm and tugged her over to me, grinning when she willingly climbed onto my lap. Her skirt rode up, but I ignored it as I wrapped my hand in the back of her hair, loving the way the soft curls felt against my skin.

Dark espresso eyes looked at me under thick lashes before they closed and her lips fluttered over mine. I pulled her closer, my tongue playfully caressing hers as she deepened the kiss and lowered herself further over my now-hard erection.

She wrapped her arms around my neck as we made out, my hands fighting the temptation to reach down and grab her ass. A soft moan escaped her lips as she pulled away for a second before crashing down over mine again.

Her fingers were cold as they brushed against my skin while she lifted my sweater and pushed it over my head. I wasn't sure how far this was going tonight, but I wasn't complaining. I had a beautiful woman who was taking the lead, and I loved it.

"You're so much hotter in person than you are in the calendar," she said, nipping my ear as she planted open-mouthed kisses along my collarbone. "I want to see more."

She reached down and worked the button and fly on my jeans before eagerly reaching in and stroking me through my boxers.

"Thank you," I moaned, letting my head fall back as I closed my eyes and focused on how she made me feel. "You're really hot, too."

"I want more," she panted, slipping her hand into the opening and rubbing my cock. "Do you want to go to my room?"

I nodded, unable to speak. She giggled as I gave her ass a hard squeeze before standing up, holding her as she wrapped her legs around my waist and held on.

"It's that one," she whispered, pointing to her room.

I opened the door and then locked it as soon as we were inside. She climbed down and immediately went to work pulling her shirt off, revealing a sexy black lace bra.

My eyes locked onto her full, round breasts, imagining how heavy they would feel in my hands.

As if reading my mind, she reached behind and unclasped her bra, pulling the fabric from her body and letting it fall to the floor.

I groaned as she stood there wearing just her skirt, her nipples hardening as she brushed her hands over them.

"Jeans off," she commanded, unzipping her skirt in the back and letting it fall to the floor. She stepped out of it, wearing nothing but black lace panties that matched the bra.

I quickly took off my jeans, grabbing a condom from my wallet before tossing everything aside. I held it between my teeth as I hooked my thumbs into the waistband of my boxers and pulled them down, watching as her eyes lit up as my cock sprung free.

"Now *that* should be in the calendar," she said, chewing her lower lip again. "We can add an extra month at the end and call it Dicktember. It'll be like Christmas, where you give me the gift of dick all month long."

"Is that so?" I asked, stepping out of my boxers and stroking my cock for her. "Well, I am in the giving mood."

"Good. Me too."

She jumped up, wrapping her legs around my waist as her hands locked behind my neck. Our mouths found each other in an instant, eagerly exploring again.

I walked back to the bed and gently laid her down, loving the way her breasts had felt against my body.

"Are you sure you want to do this?" I asked, kissing the side of her neck before allowing myself to touch her.

"Yes. I want this, Jones," she breathed.

I ran my tongue along her body, enjoying the goosebumps it left along the way. Her legs parted as she grabbed my hand and pushed it to where she wanted it. I chuckled as I kissed my way down her chest, teasing her and pulling her nipple into my mouth as my finger caressed her slit.

"Such a needy little thing, aren't you?" I teased.

She whimpered and arched her back, my finger gliding through her wetness as I pushed her panties to the side and slipped it inside. A loud gasp escaped her mouth as I moved to the other nipple, pinning her body down with the weight of mine while I inserted another finger.

I sucked harder, her breathing getting more ragged as I brushed my thumb against her clit and rubbed in a circular motion. Her nails dug into my back, scratching the skin as she leaned into my touch.

"Fuck, you're really good at this," she whimpered, her back arching deeper.

I grinned and released her nipple before moving my way down her body. If she thought I was good with my hand, she was about to see just how *great* I was with my mouth.

Right as I got to the top of her panties, I stopped and pulled my fingers out of her, laughing at how she grunted her disapproval in response.

"Lift your hips," I demanded, waiting for her to do as I asked so I could remove her panties. I didn't want anything to stand in my way of pleasuring her.

Once they were gone, I spread her legs further, licking my lips as her glistening pussy greeted me. Then I leaned in and licked her slit, loving when she reached down and grabbed my head to hold me in place. I grabbed her hips and pinned her down as I fucked her with my tongue, her arousal coating my face. I teased her with long, soft strokes as her nails dug into my skin, the sting of it only adding to my arousal.

I flicked her clit repeatedly with my tongue before pulling the swollen bud into my mouth and sucking. I could hear her panting and moaning as her body tightened around me as she got closer. Her legs began to close as she cried out, her orgasm quickly approaching.

I continued to suck her clit, eating her out as if my life depended on it. Then I felt the first spasm against my tongue as her orgasm crashed over her. I didn't release my grip on her and continued the sweet torture as she tried to buck off the bed, pulling my hair as waves of pleasure washed over her.

"FUCK!" she cried, her body going limp beneath me.

As she laid there trying to catch her breath, I leaned back and wiped my mouth with my hand as I stared down at the most beautiful girl I'd ever seen.

"Oh my God," she panted. "That was amazing."

"I'm glad you enjoyed it."

She looked down at my cock and licked her lips.

"I really want to suck that cock of yours, but I also really, really want you to fuck me senseless with it, and don't know if I'm that patient," she admitted.

"Well, your wish is my command. You know, rules of Dicktember," I teased with a wink, grabbing the condom from the bed where I had tossed it earlier. I tore it open and sheathed myself.

"How do you want it?" I asked, getting her attention as she continued to stare at it.

"Hard. Fast. Thoroughly fucked."

I nodded, grinning like a fool when I knew exactly how to achieve that.

"On your knees facing the wall," I instructed, climbing up behind her on the bed.

She looked over her shoulder and grinned at me as she rested her hands on the padded headboard.

I pushed her legs open with my knee as I lined myself up, making sure I could get as deep as I wanted to in this position. Her skin was soft against my hands as I gripped her hips and pulled her back, rubbing my cock against her ass playfully. While I also wanted to be balls deep in her tight ass, I wanted to feel her pussy first. Hopefully, there would be a round two or three if I played my cards right so that I could have both.

"You ready?" I asked, stroking myself as I gently pushed her head down to the pillow, making her ass pop up and giving me a nice view of her pussy. I reached down and ran my finger through her slit, loving the way it glistened from her arousal. Her legs parted like she was going to do the splits, opening herself up for me. She was more flexible than I had imagined, which gave me promising thoughts about other positions we could try later.

"I'm more than ready," she answered, reaching down and rubbing her finger through her wetness as she pushed mine out of the way.

"Good."

Without saying another word, I pressed my cock against her opening and pushed inside, holding my breath as her warm pussy wrapped around me. She was so fucking tight, her walls gripping me greedily as I slid in, inch by inch.

My head fell back as I let her adjust to my size, pure heaven spreading all around me.

She began moving against me, rocking back as she tried to pull me in deeper.

"Hard, Jones. I want you to fuck me hard," she whimpered.

I nodded even though she couldn't see me. Then I grabbed hold of her hips and slammed into her, the bed hitting the wall with a thud. She cried out as I did it again. And again.

Within seconds, we had the perfect rhythm between us as she met me thrust for thrust. I knew she wanted it hard, but I hadn't imagined just how rough she wanted it until the walls were shaking, and a picture fell from her nightstand, crashing to the floor.

I bit my lip and kept from moaning loudly as her pussy spasmed around me as she rubbed her clit until she came. My orgasm washed over me a few seconds later, my load quickly filling the condom.

While this might have started because Bella wanted to explore whatever this spark was between us, neither of us could have anticipated how incredible it would be once we actually fucked. There was no going back now that I had had Bella.

<u>Four</u>
Bella

Sex with Jones was better than anything I could have ever imagined. He got me off quicker than any of the Dark Vibes toys I had recently tried after they let me keep them from the photoshoot. It wasn't like they were used, having only been taken out of the package for a few photos. I was the only one who handled them, but the manager insisted I keep everything since it was already open.

We laid on my bed, completely spent and naked after an amazing fuck. For once, I didn't get up and rush to the bathroom to clean up or attempt to cover myself. With Jones, I felt comfortable, and I wasn't sure what that meant since this was so new and unexpected. I started this because I wanted to explore the chemistry I felt when we touched, but I never imagined this would be the result. Not that I was complaining. Jones was a very attractive man, and the time we'd spent together had always been fun.

"Can I tell you something?" I asked, turning my head to look at him.

"Anything."

"I don't ever do this kind of thing," I said, exhaling heavily.

He turned his head and searched my face.

"Jumping into bed with someone I'm not even dating," I answered for him with a nervous laugh. "I'm not a promiscuous girl. Never even had a one-night stand before."

"I didn't think you were," he said softly.

"I know what people around town think of me. Hell, I've been hearing it my whole life. It's like just because I'm *pretty*, I must be getting with every guy I can. Add on the whole lingerie model bit, and everyone thinks I'm just sleeping around and using my sex appeal to get what I want."

"I don't think that."

"I know," I assured him, rolling onto my side to look at him. "I'm not saying this to get pity or anything like that, but do you know how hard it is for me to date? To always have to question whether someone is actually interested in who I am as a person and not just because of what I look like. I never know how genuine someone is because everyone wants to brag about fucking the girl who takes photos with sex toys. It's like I'm a porn star in their eyes, which I'm not."

"People suck," he muttered, rolling over to face me. "I don't think that about you at all."

"That's why I wanted to do this tonight. I wanted to do it my way. To be in control. I wanted to act on this spark that I felt with you because, for once in my life, I actually felt something, and it was thrilling and exhilarating. If I initiated it, I wouldn't have to question whether there were ulterior motives, which I honestly don't think I could ever see coming from you. You're way too nice for that. But this chemistry was new and exciting, and I just wanted to feel something real for once."

"I felt it, too. But I'm glad you were the one to act on it because I probably wouldn't have ever tried to."

My brows pinched together.

"Why not?"

"I don't know." He shrugged one shoulder, propping himself up on his elbow. "I never thought a girl like you would ever be interested in a guy like me. I'm not usually one who will try to shoot my shot if I think there's a good chance to get rejected."

"How could I not be?" I asked, genuinely startled by his admission. Didn't he see how amazing of a person he was? Kindhearted and giving, always quick to help out when needed. Who wouldn't want to be with someone like that?

"I'm the talk of the town for different reasons, but still, it's not like women are parading around claiming I'm the best they've ever had. I didn't think I had anything to offer someone as wonderful as you."

"Well then, I'm glad I made the first move. But I hate to disappoint you by not telling everyone how incredible you are in bed. It's just that I don't want—"

"You don't have to explain, Bella," he said gently, interrupting me as he reached over and draped his arm over my side as his fingers lightly tickled above my ass. "I don't need you to tell anyone about what happened between us. I just need you to enjoy yourself and to trust me when I say that not only are you the best I've ever had, but I'm interested in more than just your body and gorgeous looks."

"Ditto," I giggled, feeling the warmth lick its way up my body as his hand moved down and caressed my butt.

He scooted closer, his lips feathering over mine as he massaged the plump globes before slipping a finger down the crack.

"I love your body," he murmured against my ear before nipping it. "And I can't wait to explore more of it. Especially this tight ass of yours."

I lifted a leg and brought it up over his hip, pulling myself closer to him as he continued to tease the puckered hole.

"You can have my ass," I offered seductively. "But first, I want you to fuck my mouth."

He inhaled sharply and closed his eyes as he allowed me to push him onto his back. I licked my lips and grabbed a hair tie from the nightstand, pulling my hair into a messy ponytail. I locked eyes with him before I worked my way down his body, allowing my breasts to tease his skin along the way. His cock was hard and ready for me as I gripped it in my hand and then licked the tip, loving the hiss that escaped his clenched mouth.

I lowered my mouth over his cock, taking him to the back of my throat, ignoring the gag reflux as I relaxed my jaw. He hardened in my hand as he moaned above me. I worked him with my hand, gently caressing his balls with the other one while I sucked.

He gripped my head, gently pulling my hair as I worked him with my mouth. I hollowed out my cheeks and took him further, flattening my tongue the best I could. My head bobbed up and down in the perfect rhythm while he guided me with his hand.

"Fuck, Bella," he breathed. "I'm going to come. If you don't want it in your mouth, you should pull away NOW."

Grinning the best I could with a huge cock in my mouth, I planted myself firmly against him, draining every ounce as he shot ropes of cum down the back of my throat. His deep groans were the best sounds, immediately making me wet again. Tonight was going to be a long but fun night as we tried to get our fill of each other.

34

<u>Five</u>
Jones

I woke up with an arm hanging across my chest and warm breasts pushed against my body. I didn't want to move and wake Bella, but I also really had to pee. I wanted to stay like this forever, but I knew the moment I walked out of this bedroom that might be the end of it. Bella would come to her senses and realize she could do better than me, then move on.

"Mmm," Bella moaned sleepily, letting her hand slip down to where my cock was standing at attention. "Good morning to me."

"While I would love to give you the wake-up call you deserve, I'm afraid if I don't go relieve myself, I might explode."

"Down the hall, last door on the left," she answered, allowing her arm to fall to the bed as I got up. I grabbed my pants and slid them on before pulling my shirt over my head. It was still early, so I knew it was unlikely for Lia to be up, especially after the night she had, but I still didn't want to risk her catching me sneaking to the bathroom in my underwear.

I closed the door quietly, did my business, and then made my way back to Bella's room. By the time I got back, she was out of bed and securing her hair in a messy bun on top of her head.

"Lia just got up," she explained, disappointment etched on her face.

"Oh," I said, grabbing my shoes. "Want me to sneak out?"

She scrunched her face as she thought about it.

"No, that seems a bit extreme," she said, shaking her head. "But I don't think I'm ready to explain us to anyone just yet. I kinda like having it as our little secret if that's okay with you?"

I nodded, unsure what to say.

"So, what do you want to do?" I asked, letting her take the lead.

Just then, we heard the water turn on across the hall as the shower started in the master bathroom.

"She's getting in the shower, so we should be okay. Sorry to kick you out."

"It's fine. Really."

We walked to the door, and Bella stopped as she listened, then slowly opened the door. We got to the end of the hallway and almost to the kitchen when we heard a door open and footsteps coming down the hall.

I gently shoved Bella into the kitchen and then squatted down to look at an outlet by the cabinet.

"I don't know why it keeps tripping, but we should definitely have it checked," I said, bullshitting as I felt Lia walk up to us.

"Oh, hi. I didn't realize anyone was here," she replied, holding her towel tighter against her body as I glanced over my shoulder. "I was just coming to grab my coffee before jumping in the shower."

"Didn't mean to startle you," I apologized. "I came by to check this outlet. Bella said it's been going out often and was worried it might be a fire hazard."

"I didn't know that. I just used it the other day, and it worked fine," Lia said, brows pulled together as she leaned forward. "Did you try plugging something into it, or can you tell just by looking at it?"

"We were just getting ready to plug this in," I said, standing up and reaching for a box beside me on the counter.

I heard a small gasp escape Bella's lips as she covered her face with her hands and spun around.

Lia's eyes widened as she stared at me in disbelief.

"That's what you're going to plug in?" Lia asked, cocking her head to the side as she tucked the top of her towel in further.

I looked down to find a box with a flesh-colored dildo in my hand. But it wasn't just any dildo—it was the fucking king of all dildos, measuring twelve inches long with a piercing through the tip. I swallowed hard, unsure of what to say as I continued to hold the bawdy package in my hand.

"Sorry, I must have grabbed the wrong thing," I said, clearing my throat as I set it on the counter beside me. My cheeks burned hot as embarrassment washed over me.

Lia narrowed her eyes as she looked between us.

"What's going on?" she asked. "Are you two messing around or something? Why is he here this early in the morning and trying to plug in your dildo?"

"Nope," I said, shaking my head as I stared at the floor. "Just here doing a safety check, keeping the residents of Beaumont Creek from starting unnecessary fires." I rocked back on my heels as I lied through my teeth.

"Here it is," Bella said, interrupting at the perfect moment. "Sorry about the mishap. Sometimes I forget to put work stuff away." She grabbed the box with the Dark Vibes logo across the top and pushed it back into the corner on the counter before handing me a different box with a hand mixer. Her eyes softened, and she offered a sympathetic smile while Lia wasn't looking.

"Thanks." I took it out of the box and unwrapped the cord before plugging it into the outlet. I slid the button up and turned it on. "Looks like this one is working just fine," I said, turning it off and unplugging it.

"Perfect. Good to know." Bella smiled widely, but I could see she was still nervous with how Lia continued to watch us.

"I thought you said it wasn't working?" Lia asked, studying Bella.

"I must have forgotten to turn it on." She shook her head and placed her palm on her forehead. "Silly me. Where is my head these days? Must be more tired than I thought."

"Why are you so tired?" Lia probed, arms folded over her chest.

"I don't know. Just didn't sleep well last night. Maybe too many shots?"

"I didn't sleep well either. There were a lot of loud noises, and I kept hearing this constant thumping. It would stop and then start again. It was super annoying. If I didn't know better, I would say the neighbors were up fucking all night long. But that would be hard to believe given that they're in their seventies." She snorted, rolling her eyes.

Bella's face flushed with color as she turned away and started fixing a cup of coffee.

"It was probably the neighbors," she lied, the dark liquid filling her cup. "Maybe they were exercising again? And it probably wasn't as late as you thought, given how intoxicated you were."

"Maybe. The walls are pretty thin," Lia agreed, lips pursed tightly.

"The joys of living in a duplex and sharing a wall." Bella lifted her mug and took a sip while I tried not to burst into laughter at how many lies were flying around me this morning.

"You would think things would be much quieter with having elderly neighbors," Lia muttered, grabbing her coffee from the island and heading back to the bathroom.

I exhaled heavily, relieved to be in the clear, when she suddenly stopped and turned back to look at me.

"Hey, Jones?"

"Yeah?"

"Would you mind checking the rest of the outlets before you go? I wouldn't want to risk starting a fire with a faulty outlet in a brand-new house." She locked eyes with me, telling me she read through the load of crap we just tried to feed her.

<u>Six</u>

Bella

"Where are you going?" I asked, legs curled under me on the couch as Lia rushed through the kitchen, stuffing her bag full of snacks before filling her water bottle with ice water.

"I start my clinical rotations today."

"Oh my God, how did I forget?" I pressed my palm to my head. I was so used to her being home on the weekends that it was weird to see her up and going so early on a Sunday morning. "How do you feel about it? Are you nervous?"

"I'm a mess," she admitted, forcing her shoulders down as she looked at me. "But I'm also excited about it. I'm a second-year medical student who gets to start my clinicals a few months early. I'm taking that as a sign from the universe that this is where I'm meant to be. Even though we all know it's just part of living in a small town and having to fight for scheduling time at the hospital for clinical rotations."

"You'll be in the ER, right?"

"Yeah, this one is ER, and the next is general surgery. I can't wait for that one."

"Well, break a leg," I offered, immediately scrunching my nose. "Okay, not literally. You know what I mean."

"Thanks. Be good and try not to set anything on fire while I'm gone," Lia tossed over her shoulder as she winked at me and walked out the front door.

I knew she was suspicious about what was going on between me and Jones. And I wanted to tell her about it, I really did. But there was something comforting about being able to just be myself around him and not having to worry about anyone thinking they had a say in whatever was going on between us. I had become so accustomed to everyone having an opinion—whether it was how I looked in my photos or whether I should be working with a sex toy company—that I just wanted to make decisions for myself. To be in complete and total control of something for once.

After Lia left, I got up and made myself breakfast, making sure to get myself back on track after this weekend and the extra calories I'd consumed. I was hoping that Lia would either find her one true love or take a break from dating because I couldn't handle these girls' nights out anymore.

But with her starting her clinicals, that meant she would have even less free time than before. She quit her job a few weeks ago in preparation for this, and now that her family business was up and running like a well-oiled machine, she hadn't been needed there either. She would still be putting in twelve to fourteen-hour long days with very few breaks until she finished med school, which meant I would hardly see her.

By noon, I had completed my daily workout routine and added in an extra thirty minutes of cardio because I had the time. I jumped in the shower, cleaned up, and then sat down to go through a few emails that had come through from my agent.

One was regarding a possible new job, which I was strongly considering now that Lia's income was going from steady to zilch. I was still making great money from Dark Vibes, but I wasn't sure how long they would need me. It seemed we were almost through with their entire catalog, but I hadn't heard anything more about it. I had an exclusivity agreement in my contract with them, but I was pretty sure that modeling for a new high-end boutique in town wasn't any sort of direct competition. One would have me wearing pearls and decked out in a full-length satin gown, while the other would be skimpy lingerie and thigh-high stockings.

I replied, letting her know I was available to discuss things tomorrow. Then, I opened my social media app and found myself pulling Jones' profile up. I chewed my lower lip in between my teeth as his picture loaded. It was my favorite one because his dark hair was slightly tousled, and the light hit his green eyes perfectly. Not only that, his full, plump lips drew my attention straight to them, making me yearn for how they would feel against my skin.

The worst part was that now I knew exactly how they felt, and yet I still couldn't get enough.

I closed the app and let out a frustrated breath as I got off the couch and walked into the kitchen. I meant to grab a glass of ice water but spotted the box with the pierced dildo from yesterday morning sitting on the counter.

Deciding that I had enough of being sexually frustrated this morning, I grabbed it and headed to my bedroom, closing the door behind me.

<u>Seven</u>

Jones

"Thanks for coming in today," Captain said as I put my stuff into my locker. "I wouldn't have expected the entire B shift to be out sick, but it appears they all got food poisoning last night."

I schooled my features, trying not to laugh that, for once, I wasn't responsible for it.

"It's not a problem," I assured him.

"Most of A shift can come in today, but we have a few guys from C shift available if needed."

"Sounds good." I closed my locker and headed out to start checking the truck and doing an inventory count while we waited for the rest of the guys to get there. A few of them were already out there, so I gave a nod to Capshaw and Rodriguez and then got to work.

An hour later, we were all piled up in the truck, heading to the local nursing home to visit with the residents and see the new facility that had been built with money raised from a recent fundraiser. As we were driving, a call came over the radio requesting assistance from an elderly woman who was hearing sounds of distress from her neighbor's house.

Capshaw and I exchanged a worried glance when the address came through as Lia and Bella's. Rodriquez stepped on the gas, but it felt like we couldn't get there fast enough.

"Alright, Rodriquez and Thompson, check in with the residents that called it in. Capshaw and Jones report to the neighbor's house," Captain directed. Nate was close to his team, so it wasn't any surprise that he didn't ask us to stand back, knowing that it was possibly Capshaw's sister who was in trouble.

We rushed to the front door and I waited for Capshaw to pull out a key and let himself in, but instead, he pounded on the door and yelled, "Beaumont Creek Fire Department. Open the door."

I worked my jaw back and forth, fighting the urge to break down the door and rush inside. Who knew what was going on or if Bella or Lia were injured? What if one of them fell and hit their head? What if they were unconscious? What if someone had broken into the house and attacked them? Sure, Beaumont Creek didn't have a high crime rate, but that didn't mean we were completely free of it.

I opened my mouth to ask him about a key but snapped it shut when he gave me a warning look and pounded his fist again.

"This is Beaumont Creek Fire Department. Please open the door, or we will break it dow—"

"Hey, what's up?" A very breathless Bella said, answering the door wearing nothing but a thin tank top that allowed her puckered nipples to poke through and a pair of cotton booty shorts. She held the door against her body, trying to shield herself.

Capshaw looked away, clearly uncomfortable by what she was wearing and how it looked like she had been inside having hot, wild sex.

"Umm, your neighbor called regarding a woman in distress," he explained, looking past me to the house where Rodriguez and Thompson were talking to a woman with curlers in her hair and a robe tied tightly around her waist.

Bella leaned forward and peeked around the stuccoed wall to see.

"Sorry about that," she said, wincing as she pulled her lower lip between her teeth. "Everything is fine here."

She stepped back and opened the door, inviting us in.

"You're welcome to take a look around," she said, folding her arms over her chest, which did nothing but remind me of how her nipples felt in my mouth a few nights ago.

I tried to discreetly adjust myself as I felt the strain of my hardening cock against the fabric of my pants. We didn't have our turnout gear on as we were heading to a nursing home and not an active call, though it would have been helpful to help hide my hard-on.

"Is Lia home?" Capshaw asked, walking through the living room and kitchen, checking everything was alright.

"No," Bella said, shaking her head. "She started her first day of her clinical rotations this morning. It's just me."

"And you're not in distress?" he asked, still refusing to look at her.

"Nope. Not in the least. Must have been something else she heard." Bella shrugged.

"She said it sounded like a woman crying out in pa—" I started, then stopped when I realized where this was going.

Bella's cheeks flushed as she tucked a strand of hair behind her ear. I turned away so I didn't continue to embarrass her and found the empty package of the flesh-colored dildo from yesterday morning on the counter. It was open and missing the dildo.

Capshaw must have noticed it at the same time because he grabbed his radio and very quietly reported back that everything was fine there and that it was a false alarm.

"Well, it appears this was a false alarm," Capshaw replied awkwardly. "Sorry for the intrusion, Bella."

I offered her a smile, but it fell awkwardly on my lips. I shoved my hands in my pockets and was ready to follow Capshaw out.

"Sorry you guys were called out for nothing," she said softly.

"Well, I wouldn't say it was for nothing," he remarked casually. "I did notice a damaged extension cord by the TV, which poses a fire hazard. Jones will stay back and assist with that."

I pulled my brows together in confusion.

"I will?"

"Yes. We take safety very seriously in the Beaumont Creek Fire Department, and I cannot, in good faith, allow you to leave knowing that the frayed cord could spark a fire. Please stay behind and deal with that."

I stepped closer to him and furrowed my brow in confusion.

"Are you okay?" I asked, wondering if the call being for his sister's house had done something to freak him out. "It was a false alarm; there's nothing to be worried about."

"I'm not worried about it being a false alarm, Jones. I'm worried about taking you to the nursing home with that thing sticking out and all of the residents fighting over who gets to grab it. Or worse yet—having someone lose an eye. Stay here and deal with whatever is going on between the two of you. Once you're *good*, you can meet up with us later."

I looked down to notice my erection had only gotten worse, jutting straight out. I rolled my head back on my neck and closed my eyes, wondering if I could be any more mortified.

50

Eight
Bella

I wasn't sure what was more embarrassing—having my neighbors call for help because they could hear me moaning through the stupidly thin walls or the fact that Jones was told not to go back to work until his erection went away.

I hadn't expected to see him today, but in all fairness, it wasn't like I was planning for a visit from the local fire department. If I had been, I would have thrown on a bra and fixed my hair before opening the door and seeing the mortified look on Lia's brother's face when he realized what was really going on.

"Everything okay?" I asked nervously, chewing my nail as Jones closed the door and locked it.

He lowered his head as his shoulders rose and fell with the breath he exhaled.

I wrapped my arms tighter around myself and waited for him to turn and face me. His schooled expression helped keep me from glancing down to see if he was still hard. I had no business looking, but then again, I didn't have much restraint now that I knew what he was packing and what he could do with it.

He nodded his head, still not saying anything.

"I'm really sorry—" I started but snapped my mouth shut when he held his hand up to stop me.

I pressed my lips together, fighting the urge to speak.

"What were you doing, Bella?" he asked, his voice sounding strangled, as if his throat was too tight to allow the words to come out.

I swallowed hard, looking down at the floor.

"Nothing. Just moving some furniture around," I lied, toeing a line in the carpet.

"Really?"

I could hear the change in his tone as he stepped closer, now merely inches away from me. The heat from his body sending heat waves washing over mine.

"Moving furniture makes you moan loud enough for your neighbors to call for help?"

I kept my head down, embarrassment washing over me as I recalled exactly what I had been thinking about when I came hard enough to lose control.

"Does moving furniture make your nipples hard, too?" he pressed, lifting my chin with his finger and forcing my eyes up to meet his. "Or were you doing something *else*?"

He leaned into me, the feel of his erection brushing against my stomach. I looked into his eyes and saw the same desire I had seen there the other night. Without giving it a second thought, I jumped into his arms, wrapped my legs around his waist, and pressed my lips against his.

A deep, guttural growl erupted from his throat as he deepened the kiss and gripped my ass as he carried me down the hallway and to my bedroom. He kicked the door shut and locked it before setting me on the bed and standing in front of me.

"Do you want me to move some furniture for you, or are you already wet for me?" he teased, pulling his shirt over his head and tossing it to the floor.

"Why don't you check for yourself?" I offered, lying back on my elbows and letting my legs fall to the side. I knew my shorts were short enough to let him see my bare pussy and how wet it was.

He sighed heavily, chewing his lower lip while shaking his head as he slid off his pants and boxer briefs. His cock jutted up to his stomach, a drop of precum on the tip glistening in the light.

My body hummed with anticipation as my sex ached, the tension already building up.

His fingers wrapped around his dick, stroking slowly along the base as I watched. While I had enjoyed the toy from Dark Vibes earlier, nothing would ever compare to the real thing, especially when it was Jones. He may not know how to cook, but that didn't mean he wasn't packing the heat where it mattered.

I slid a finger down and parted my folds, desperate for the attention he was stalling on giving my needy clit. I closed my eyes and moaned as it glided effortlessly through my arousal.

"Is this what you were doing when your neighbors called?" he asked, leaning down to get a better look as I fingered myself. "Or were you putting that thing to good use?" He nodded to the dildo sitting on my nightstand.

"Do you want the truth?" My eyes fluttered open so I could see him nod.

"Show me."

My legs trembled as my fingers brushed against my clit before I pulled them out. He grabbed the toy, handing it to me as he watched with such intensity that it made me even more turned on.

"Or you could do it for me," I offered, suddenly feeling shy.

"Nope. I want to watch. I want to see what was going on, what had you screaming so loud that you grabbed the attention of your neighbors. Show me how you fucked yourself with that, Bella."

"It's a lot harder with an audience," I admitted. "Though, at least I don't have to picture you naked since you already are." I let out an awkward laugh.

"How about I'll show you what I do when you're not around, and you show me what you were doing?" He sat down in the chair by the window and slowly began stroking himself again as he watched me hold the toy in my hand.

Suddenly, the toy felt heavier as I held it, the weight of what I was about to do sending chills through me. It was both thrilling and nerve-wracking as I considered sharing this side of me with Jones, but I also felt a rush of confidence wash over me when I saw how he was looking at me.

I set the toy down while I took off my shorts, then got comfy on the bed, positioning myself where he could easily see. I closed my eyes and grabbed the toy, my finger brushing against the piercing on the tip before rubbing it against my clit.

I hissed out a breath, loving the way my nipples hardened as I slid the toy slowly inside me. It was bigger than anything I had ever had before, but I could hear by the sounds Jones was making that he was as turned on by this as I was. My back arched as I lifted my hips and pushed it in further, shuddering as I imagined Jones fucking me with it.

I kept going, keeping a steady pace so I didn't come right away. I was close enough already, but I was enjoying this with Jones and wasn't ready for it to end.

"Fuck," he grunted, startling me as my eyes flew open and my hand stopped with the toy still inside me.

"What's wrong?" I asked, looking around the room.

"I can't do this." He got up and crossed the room in a matter of seconds, grabbing the toy from me and taking over fucking me with it as he pushed my hand out of the way.

I grinned as I watched his eyes fixate on my pussy, studying the way it swallowed the toy every time he moved it.

"I've never been so fucking jealous of anything in my life," he muttered. "But now I'm determined to make you come better than this fucker did."

I giggled but stopped when he suddenly yanked it out of my body, making sure to brush the ring against my clit.

Everything happened so quickly, and before I knew it, his dick was wrapped in a condom, and he was pushing so deep inside me that I could swear I saw stars.

"I may not be pierced, but I can fuck you better than that toy," he growled, lowering himself as he pulled out and then slammed back into me.

"Fuck," I cried, closing my eyes and grabbing the back of my thighs to hold them up while he kept up the delicious torture of pounding into my pussy.

"Keep doing that," I begged. "I'm so close."

He said something, maybe dirty talk of some sort, but I couldn't focus on the words coming out of his mouth once his finger dipped between us and began rubbing my clit. The next thing I knew, stars were shooting behind my eyes as I came undone and fell into a world of pure ecstasy.

Nine

Jones

When I arrived at the firehouse, it was empty while the others finished at the nursing home. I had checked in with Captain while I caught a ride share back and he said to go ahead and report to the station. I was thankful that he didn't ask questions about why I was held back at Bella's house—though I knew Capshaw had already filled him in. And given that no one knew what was happening between Bella and me, I knew Capshaw probably made up some crazy story that would embarrass the hell out of me later when Nate teased me about it.

I finished cleaning the kitchen and pulled the ground beef out of the fridge so I could start dinner. There were few things I could *actually cook*, and thankfully, tacos were one of them. I had yet to ruin those, so I grabbed a skillet and started cooking the meat while I fetched a seasoning packet out of the cabinet. I tore it open and dumped it into the pan on top of the meat while using the spatula to break it into smaller pieces.

A few minutes later, the door opened, and voices carried down the hallway as the guys headed toward the kitchen.

"What's that smell?" Capshaw asked as he came in, looking over my shoulder.

"I'm making tacos for dinner."

I stirred the meat around a few more times before reaching for the seasoning packet to throw away. Before I could grab it, Capshaw's hand darted out and got it first, a smirk gracing his lips as he looked at it.

"What's that look for?" I asked, cocking my head while scowling.

"What did you say you were making?" he asked, holding the package up for the guys gathered behind him to read.

"Tacos. Why? Do you suddenly have a problem with them?"

"No," he insisted, shaking his head as his lips curled into a smile. "I don't have a problem with *tacos*. We all know I love tacos. But, I do have a problem with whatever that is you're making."

He nodded to the pan and slapped the packet against my chest, patting my shoulder a few times before walking off and sitting at the long dining table with the guys as he chuckled. I pulled it down and frowned when I saw what it was. Instead of grabbing the packet for taco seasoning, I had grabbed a brown gravy one.

"Shit," I muttered, tossing my head back and closing my eyes. "How do I fix this?"

"You can't. That's why I don't use packets, my friend. All of my seasoning comes from the heart," Rodriguez said, patting his chest.

"Or whatever your wife tells you to make," Nate said, sitting at the head of the table.

"That too," Rodriguez conceded, joining them. "But she never steers me wrong. That's why we've been married for so long."

"Either that, or she just thinks it's too much work to divorce you," Capshaw teased, ducking when Rodriguez tossed something at his head.

I grabbed my phone out of my pocket, found the number I was looking for, and pressed the call button.

"What did you burn this time?" Dylan asked.

He'd been my friend long enough to know this about me. Hell, it seemed to be the *only* thing people knew about me.

"Nothing, but I'm about to," I admitted, turning the heat down on the meat. "Umm. I hate to bug you, but is Calli there by chance? I have a cooking-related question."

"Yeah, hold on."

I pulled the phone away from my ear as the background noise got louder. Finally, it stopped and Calli came on the line.

"Hey, Jones. What's up?" Calli was one of the nicest people I had ever met—though technically, we had yet to meet since she lived across the country in Montana with my friend Dylan. Still, she was always willing to help me with cooking-related dilemmas—which I tended to have a lot of.

"I was trying to make tacos," I started, letting out a heavy sigh.

"Did you forget to take the liner from the meat package out again?"

"No, I remembered to do that. This time, I grabbed the wrong seasoning packet, and instead of putting taco seasoning in, I added a packet of brown gravy."

"Oh my," she whispered with a giggle.

"I know, I know. What are my options? Is there any way to save this?"

"You can turn it into beef stroganoff," she suggested. "You'll need some egg noodles, sour cream, and cream of mushroom soup, as well as some seasonings. Do you have the other stuff?"

"Hold on, let me check."

I rested the phone between my ear and shoulder as I checked the pantry. I grabbed the items she asked for, struggling to hold everything in my hands as she continued to give me directions over the phone. I set everything on the counter and felt the tension in my neck when I realized how much was going to be required to pull this meal off after all.

"Do you want to FaceTime me?" she offered as I added everything in and did exactly what she said.

"I think I got it, but thank you. If you hear on the news that a fire station comes down with food poisoning two nights in a row, you'll know it was me."

"You gave everyone food poisoning last night?!" she gasped.

"No," I said with a laugh. "That one wasn't my fault. But we got called in today because the crew from last night all got it. I'm hoping I can make it through dinner tonight without making anyone sick."

"Best of luck. Call back if you need anything."

"Will do, thanks, Calli."

I hung up the phone and stared at the stove, praying for divine intervention to make tonight's meal an actual success.

****

"This is good, Jones," Capshaw said, pushing a forkful of noodles into his mouth.

"Thank you," I replied quietly, lowering my head as heat flamed across my cheeks and spread over my ears. It was still an odd feeling for me to accept any sort of praise, given I grew up most of my life without it. It was easier—and more comforting—to hear what I had done wrong and to be reassured about what a fuck up I was.

"Where did you learn how to make beef stroganoff?" Nate asked, a genuine interest reflected on his face.

"My friend Dylan's girlfriend is an amazing cook and runs this fun restaurant in Whiskey Mountain. I've chatted with her a handful of times about cooking, and she usually comes to the rescue. When I told her what I had done with the seasonings, it was her idea to turn it into beef stroganoff. I'm honestly surprised it came together and was edible." I laughed nervously.

"Not to be a dick, but me too," Capshaw agreed with a grin. "It was starting to look a little worrisome when I saw you smell the sour cream a dozen times to see if it was still good.”

“I don’t ever eat that stuff. How was I supposed to know?” I shrugged and took another bite before reaching for the garlic bread I had accidentally burned. At least one part of the meal was edible, and no one really cared about the bread as they devoured the stroganoff. It was Calli’s idea to add the bread as a side, which was needed given how quickly the stroganoff was going.

“Well, either way, it all worked out. Thanks for dinner.” Nate stood up and cleared his plate before loading it into the dishwasher.

Soon, the room started to clear out, leaving Capshaw and me as the last two.

“So, what’s going on with you and Bella?” he asked, cutting straight to the chase as I added the dishwasher pod and pressed start.

“Umm,” I hesitated, folding my arms over my chest as I leaned against the counter. “I don’t know. We’ve hooked up a few times but haven’t labeled it. She doesn’t want to tell anyone about us right now, but I don’t know what that means for the future. Whether we’ll be hook-up buddies or something more, who knows.”

“What do you want?”

I raised an eyebrow and pinned him with a look. He knew what I wanted with Bella. It wasn’t like I could hide anything from Capshaw, even if I wanted to. I had only been obsessing over her for who knew how long now.

“So why don’t you tell her?”

"Tell her what?"

"That you have feelings for her and want more than a no-strings-attached fling."

"And what? Scare her off? No way."

"So you'd rather act like you're good with just hooking up when you really want more than that? That's not fair to you, Jones."

"Yeah, but it's not fair to push her into a relationship either. If she doesn't want that level of commitment right now, that's fine. I'll take whatever she gives me."

"And what if you're not the only guy she's doing that with?" he challenged, making my veins heat as the blood rushed through them at the thought.

I swallowed hard, forcing down the bile before I answered.

"I guess we'll cross that bridge when we come to it. She didn't mention anything about seeing anyone else, so I'm not going to jump down rabbit holes and assume she's going to start."

He lowered his head and shook it.

"That's your call. I'd just hate to see you get hurt."

"What makes you think I will?" I asked, suddenly feeling defensive.

"You're a nice guy, Jones. It's always the nice guys who get screwed, and unless it's literally—I don't want that for you. You deserve better and shouldn't be afraid to tell her that. It's not that hard to agree to be with someone if you're interested in seeing where things can go. I'm just saying, have a talk with her and make sure you're both on the same page before you get in any deeper. At least draw a line on whether or not you guys are allowed to see other people."

He pushed off the counter and walked away, leaving me alone with this nagging, ugly feeling clawing inside my chest.

Ten

Bella

"Hey, how are things going with the clinical rotation?" I asked, pouring cereal into a bowl as Lia entered the kitchen. It had been a few days since she had started, and our schedules hadn't lined up enough for us to sit down and talk. By the time she got home every night, I was already in bed since I had such an early morning routine I liked to stick to.

"Ugh. It sucks," she muttered.

"Why? What happened?" I frowned as I poured a splash of milk into the bowl and grabbed a spoon. I hopped onto the barstool and studied how her brow furrowed deeper as she thought about it.

"I HATE the attending I've been getting assigned to. He's such a pompous ass, and all of the girls are practically in heat around him. It's stupid. I wish I could get assigned to someone who doesn't make my blood boil the way it does when he's around."

"I'm sorry. That sucks. Have you talked to anyone about getting moved?"

"Not yet," she sighed, sitting beside me with her bowl of cereal. "I don't want to be a bitch and make waves right away. The last thing I need is to get myself on the bad list where no one wants to work with me. I'm going to just have to ride it out and hope that I can get moved to general surgery before I kill him."

My eyebrows rose as she smirked to herself, likely envisioning what said murder might look like.

"Try not to do anything stupid to get you kicked out of the program," I warned.

"I won't. I promise. But today is my only day off, so I already made plans for us to go to Tipsy Taco for dinner tonight. Kensy is on board, but I'm sure she'll bring my brother with her. Want to invite Jones, or should I have Capshaw?"

I started choking on the bite I took, covering my mouth with my hand to keep from spitting milk out.

"Why would I invite him?" I asked, reaching for the napkins to avoid looking at her.

"Why wouldn't you? It seems like the least you could do after all the extra security he's provided around here lately. What with the outlets he checked and the call he came out for on Sunday. Seems like he's been a little *busy* around here, tending to *stuff*." Her smirk grew even bigger as she lifted her spoon to her mouth and studied my reaction.

I lowered my head and shook it.

"How long have you known?" I asked, cutting straight to the point.

"The second I saw him here Saturday morning. I knew you were lying when I mentioned the loud noises and banging on the wall, and you blamed the neighbors. Did you know your cheeks blush the faintest shade of crimson when you're lying? It's really quite adorable."

"Why didn't you just come out and say something?"

"Because it's much more fun to watch you squirm. Plus, I kinda got a kick out of seeing Jones try to act like nothing was happening. The way he studied that outlet so intently as if it held all the answers of the universe. But I gotta admit—I lost my shit after I left when I kept picturing the look on his face when he held up your dildo when he was looking for something to test the outlet with. That was priceless."

I covered my face with my hands, hoping I wasn't turning another shade of red, even though she would enjoy it more than she should.

"But I think the bigger—and more important—question is, why didn't you tell me you were seeing him?" Her voice changed, and when I lifted my head, I was met with the softest eyes looking at me.

"I wasn't ready to tell anyone about it yet." I shrugged. "It wasn't like we had planned it or anything. Things kinda just happened."

"Friday night?"

I nodded.

"We touched, and there was this electricity between us that I had never felt before, Lia. And so I made the move before he could. I think it was just the thought of not wanting to miss out on whatever connection we had between us but also wanting to be in control of whatever might happen to us. I'm tired of questioning whether a guy is really into me for me or just wants to brag and say he hooked up with a lingerie model. It's exhausting, and I hate that I never know anyone's true intentions."

She smiled softly as she reached over and gently squeezed my hand.

"I get it. I really do."

"I wish that wasn't such a huge part of my life right now. That I wasn't labeled as something just because of the work I do. It's not like I'm a sex worker or anything. Not that there's anything wrong with being a sex worker," I added, now stumbling over my words. "I just wish that people didn't feel the need to judge and label anyone to begin with. Just mind your business and do whatever makes you happy."

"So, what does Jones think of all this? Is he okay with you guys not telling anyone about it right now?"

"He says he is. He's been great about all of it, and the funny thing is that I don't get that same vibe from him that I get from other guys."

"What do you mean?"

"With Jones, everything just feels different—but in a good way. I feel like I could work at a fast-food joint, and he would still treat me the same way. He doesn't act like it's a big deal that I do what I do. The only thing he's gotten mad about so far was a toy I had from Dark Vibes."

"He doesn't like your toys?" Lia asked with a frown as she held her spoon in front of her, too consumed with this news to take a bite.

"No," I said with a laugh. "He doesn't mind the toys. We've played with a few of them already. He got upset with the pierced dildo and said he had never been so jealous in his life as he was over a toy that was making me moan like that. Then he insisted on proving that he could make me come better than the toy."

"And did he?" Her eyebrows lifted as she waited.

I closed my eyes and nodded, remembering exactly how incredible he had been in making me come harder than I ever had before.

"You're so fucking lucky," she said with a heavy sigh before setting her spoon down and lifting her bowl to drink the milk from it.

"I'm not going to lie; it's been pretty great having the most incredible, mind-blowing sex of my life," I admitted.

"At least one of us is. I'd be lucky to find someone to give me mediocre sex, let alone someone who can locate my clit. I swear, if some of your toys start going missing, it's not my fault. But don't worry, I'll only steal the new ones."

"Want me to shop Dark Vibes for your birthday?" I offered, joining her at the sink as we washed our dishes before loading them into the dishwasher.

"I won't say no to that. Maybe when I have a few hours free, I can use them for stress relief while working 80 hours a week and with someone I despise."

"Consider it done," I said with a laugh.

"Alright. I'm going to go shower and clean up. Text Jones and invite him tonight," she said over her shoulder.

"I don't know," I objected, pulling my lower lip between my teeth.

"Why not?" She paused in the doorway, frowning.

"I just don't know if it's the best idea. We're keeping things casual between us, and if I invite him, won't that give him the wrong message? Like I'm interested in more than that if I ask him on a date?"

"This guy is giving you the best sex of your life and makes you *feel* something no one else has, Bella. Don't you think that alone is enough to get out of your head and allow yourself to date him?"

"It's hard," I admitted. "I'm scared to do that."

"Why?"

"Because if I lower my walls and allow this to be something real between us, I'm the one who is going to get hurt. It's happened so many times already. What if making this a real relationship makes the magic I've felt with him disappear? I don't know if I'm ready for that yet."

"What if it only makes it better?" she countered.

I worried my lip between my teeth as I considered that.

"Look, I've known Jones for a while, and I can tell you that men like him don't come around often. If you like him the way you say you do, then you owe it to him to give this thing a chance. What if he's just as worried about getting hurt as you are, Bella? And the fact that he is okay with keeping this thing between you guys a secret because that's what you want should prove to you that he's not worried about people knowing he's dating a lingerie model. He's not like the other guys, so please stop treating him like he is. Give this a chance, or you're going to regret it when he realizes he deserves someone who really wants to be with him and walks away."

She smiled softly and then walked away, leaving me to process her words.

<u>Eleven</u>

Jones

I was cleaning up breakfast when I heard my phone buzz on the counter. I folded the towel I had been using and set it on the side of the sink before grabbing my phone.

Bella: Hi, we're all going to Tipsy Taquito tonight. Would you like to join us?

My cheeks burned as the smile stretched across my face as I texted out my response.

Me: That depends. Who is going, and do I have to sit by Capshaw?

Bella: The usual. Me, Lia, Kensy, Capshaw, and hopefully you. I'll save you a seat by me if you want to come.

Me: What time?

Bella: Lia wants to get there early for happy hour. Four?

Me: Sounds good. I'll be there.

Bella: It's a date (kissing face emoji)

I felt flutters dance in my stomach as I read her text again. Was this her way of asking me out on a date, even though our friends would be there too? I tried not to think too hard about it as I finished my morning chores and jumped in the shower.

The day dragged on as I waited for four o'clock to come around. It was supposed to be my last day at work, but since we got called in on Sunday, everyone agreed to adjust the schedule from there, and we worked Monday as the last day of our 48 hours on. I was off for the next three days and found myself obsessing over ways to spend time with Bella.

I hadn't been able to stop thinking about her, but more importantly, I couldn't get what Capshaw said out of my head. I wanted to be with Bella, but I didn't want to push her to be in a committed relationship with me if she wasn't ready. It felt different with her, and I would rather have whatever she wanted to give me than ask for more.

By noon, I was going stir-crazy, so I grabbed my wallet and keys and headed out the door. I was in line at Surf 'N Shack when I felt someone bump their shoulder against mine.

"I heard you made quite the beef stroganoff," Abby said, smiling at me.

"Hey, Abby," I replied, pulling my arm around her shoulders to hug her. "How are you?"

"Good, though a little jealous of this dish you made that Nate hasn't stopped talking about." She laughed lightly.

"Well, I'm glad he liked it, but don't give me too much credit," I said with a chuckle. "I was trying to make tacos."

"You turned tacos into stroganoff?" She turned her head up and looked quizzically at me.

"I used a brown gravy seasoning packet instead of taco seasoning. When I realized my mistake, I called my friend Dylan, who put me on the phone with his girlfriend, Callie. She is a cooking genius, much like you, and she saved the day by helping me turn it into the stroganoff."

"I think I like her already."

Abby walked with me through the line as we waited to place our orders.

"Are you sitting down for lunch or heading back to Rockin' Rooster?" I asked once we were next in line.

"Unfortunately, I've gotta get back. I'm just grabbing food before Sherry leaves. We're short-handed today, so I'm working a double shift since Nate has the day off. Total blessing in disguise we weren't expecting, but having him work on Sunday and shifting his days off this week is really helping."

"I'm sorry. I hope things get better for you."

"Thanks, me too. We should be better soon. Just a stomach bug going around that's taking out most of my team."

We got to the counter and went to separate registers. I was going to pay for her lunch, but she walked off before I could. Once her order was placed, she grabbed her ticket and waved as she stepped to the side to wait for it.

I was still waiting for mine to be placed when I saw Capshaw come out of the back and grin at me. He stood next to the kid struggling to ring me up and pressed a few buttons on the screen. The kid's eyes lit up as he looked over at Capshaw.

"Family discount," he said, then pressed a few more buttons and handed me a receipt.

We stepped to the side as the kid continued to stare in disbelief. He was new—though I wasn't sure how long he'd been there given that he didn't seem to know how to ring people up. Another kid came out from the kitchen and took his place at the register. He shook his head and headed to the back before returning a few seconds later with cleaning supplies to clear the tables.

"You working here today?" I asked, pressing my cup against the metal lever to fill it with ice.

"Na, I just came in to check on things and say hi to my parents. They've got things covered—for the most part," he said wearily as he watched the kid who had been ringing me up wander through the restaurant, trying to clear plates from people who were still eating.

"I wasn't that bad, was I?" I asked, cringing as I watched.

"Nope. Not even close." He patted my back and walked with me to a table.

"You having lunch here?" I asked, sitting by the window as he sat opposite me.

"I wasn't going to, but I have some time, so why not? What did you get?"

"My usual, fish and chips."

"Sounds good. I'll be back."

He hopped up and headed to the back as I sat there, feeling bad for the kid still stumbling through the room, unsure of what to do.

I sympathized with him because I had spent so many years feeling the same way.

Twelve
Bella

"Why am I so nervous?" I whispered loudly, rubbing my hands together as I tried to expel the anxious energy radiating through me. My eyes quickly scanned the crowd, trying to spot Jones. We'd gotten to Tipsy Taquito twenty minutes early—mainly because I forced Lia out the door with one shoe on and one in her hand so we could get here before anyone else.

"Because you're going to see your new *boyfriend*," she sang, grimacing when my elbow nudged her in the ribs.

"Stop it," I warned, scanning the room again. "He's not my boyfriend."

We had gotten lucky and snagged a long table in the back, which was nice since we usually ended up crammed into one of the small booths by the time we got there.

I sat in the middle with Lia on one side, knowing Jones would take the other. It made sense that would be where he would sit since Capshaw and Kensy would want to sit together and there wouldn't be room on our side. But not only that—I had boldly told him he could sit by me this morning when we were texting.

But 7:00 am Bella was a totally different person than 3:45 pm Bella. 3:45 Bella was a total hot mess and regretted everything she had agreed to this morning.

My stomach turned and did some weird flip thing when the door opened, and I waited to see who was coming in. My mouth went cotton dry as my palms started sweating, but once Jones and I locked eyes, all of that faded. I felt my shoulders relax and my breathing even out as he made his way toward us.

Lia elbowed me in the side and nodded—as if I hadn't already seen him. Hell, I don't think I noticed anyone else in the room at that point. It was all a blur except for the handsome man wearing a fitted t-shirt that hugged the perfectly defined body I'd had the pleasure of licking and teasing a few days ago. Now it felt like ages as my thighs clenched together, trying to force away the sensations lingering between them.

"Hey," he said, waving at me and Lia as he pulled out the chair beside me and sat down.

It felt a little awkward not hugging him, but I was thankful that he respected my wishes to keep our relationship a secret for a little while longer by not expecting one. I reached down and nervously tugged at the hem of my skirt, needing something to distract me and the million thoughts racing through my head.

"How's it going, Jones?" Lia asked, leaning around me to see him.

"It's good. How are you?"

"Good. Thankful for a night off before I go back to *hell*."

I leaned back and listened the best I could while Lia talked about her clinicals, but I couldn't keep my attention focused on the conversation. Not when I felt his hand gently brush against my thigh as he reached under the table to pick up the napkin I accidentally dropped. I couldn't ignore how his fingers felt against my skin or the heat trail they left behind. But now wasn't the time to think about the release I desperately needed.

"Hey, guys, sorry we're late," Kensy said, her cheeks flushed and hair slightly messed up as she accepted the seat Capshaw pulled out for her.

Lia raised an eyebrow and glared at them.

"Stop it with the dirty looks," Capshaw said, sitting down. "You'd be late too if you had a fiancé as hot as mine."

"She's one of my best friends, so yeah, she's smoking hot. But you're my brother, which makes it disgusting to even think about. Come to think of it—she might be able to do better than you," Lia said, getting the jabs toward her brother started early.

"Better watch it," he warned. "No one can do better than me, can they, baby?" He reached over and lifted Kensy's chin with his finger, directing her face to his, where he planted a kiss on her lips.

"Ugh, get a room," Lia groaned.

"We would, but we thought it would be rude to stand you up for dinner," Capshaw replied, not bothering to look at his sister as he stared deeply into his fiancé's eyes.

"I'm starving, so I'm going to go order," I said, hoping to break the tension. I stood up and almost bumped into Jones as he joined me. "Sorry." I shook my head, trying to clear the fog creeping over me again.

"Not a problem. I'm starving, too. Mind if I join you?" His voice was lower than normal, and I could see the fire burning in his eyes as he gently reached for my elbow and escorted me around the table.

We walked up to the line together, my fingers itching to reach over and grab his.

"Do you know what you want?" he asked, standing so close I could smell the scent of his cologne.

"Yes." I looked up and licked my lips, wondering if he was as deeply impacted as I was. "You."

He nodded and gave it some thought, apparently not catching that there wasn't a question mark at the end of my sentence.

"I think I'm going to mix it up tonight and do the combo fajitas. I usually stick to the chicken chimichanga, but I think trying something new might be good for me," he said, nodding to himself.

"That's not what I meant," I muttered, lifting my fingers to move the thin gold chain around my neck. It was my favorite necklace, but it was so light and delicate that I often worried I would lose it, so I didn't wear it often. I lined the heart charm up in the center and then lowered my hand before I broke the chain by fidgeting with it.

"I know," he answered, looking straight ahead instead of at me. "But if I would have responded to that the way I wanted to, I would already have you bent over one of these tables and would be balls deep inside you. I don't think anyone wants to see that, and I know you're not ready to tell anyone about us, so that's how I'm distracting myself as my balls ache from the release I desperately need, Bella. If I think about fajitas, I might get lucky and stop thinking about how good you would taste on my tongue as I lift your skirt and bury my head between your thighs."

My body trembled at his words as goosebumps erupted over my skin.

We moved forward and didn't say anything to each other after that. What was there to say anyway—no matter what I tried to say, there would be the one thing I wanted to say but couldn't. Even though I wanted to be with Jones and see what this thing between us could be, there was no way I could verbalize that yet. My throat swelled up and closed every single time I thought about it.

By the time we ordered our food and returned to the table, the others were getting up and heading to place theirs, which left us by ourselves again.

It wouldn't be such a bad thing if I weren't trying to fight the urge to attack him and ride him at the table. *Talk about a way to burn some calories and work up an appetite before dinner*. But that wasn't appropriate, and thinking about it only made things worse for me.

"What are you doing after dinner?" he asked lowly, looking up to make sure everyone else was still in line.

"I don't have plans. I'm probably calling it a night early since I have to get up early and squeeze in an extra cardio session to burn off the calories from dinner tonight. You?"

"No plans either." He shrugged. "But if you want to come over, I know a few ways we can work off some calories if you're interested."

I pulled my lip between my teeth and bit down sharply to avoid making a fool of myself as I squeezed my thighs together under the table again.

"What did you have in mind?" I asked coyly, turning to face him so I could lower my voice.

"Well, I have this excellent running trail behind my house. We could go for a run. Or I just got a new bike; we could go for a ride."

"That's not the kind of ride I had in mind," I said, looking away as I kept my voice low enough for only him to hear.

"What kind did you have in mind?"

He leaned toward me and rested his elbow on the table, shielding us from the nosey women at the table across from us.

"The kind where I ride your cock until we both come."

"That's funny; I was thinking the same thing but didn't want to come off as a pervert," he said, leaning back slightly as I inhaled sharply, trying to get more oxygen to my brain.

"Then I say we eat fast, fake food poisoning, and get the hell out of here as soon as possible," I replied quickly as I saw everyone heading back to the table. "Otherwise, I'm going to ride you here and now."

He covered his mouth behind his hand as he chuckled deeply.

Thirteen

Jones

"So, this is the living room," I said as I guided Bella into my house.

We ate quicker than I had expected, but what was more surprising was that everyone bought our story of Bella not feeling well and me taking her home. Lia and Capshaw didn't seem the slightest bit suspicious, which made me think Lia already knew about us as well. But the confusion on Kensy's face said she was about to get all the gossip after we left.

"It's beautiful," Bella said before turning around and jumping into my arms. Her legs wrapped tightly around my waist as her hands locked behind my head. My lips parted and accepted her eager tongue as it slid inside, her mouth capturing the moan that escaped mine.

"Do you want to see the rest?" I joked as my hands gripped her ass and slid the fabric of her skirt up to give me better access.

"Not unless it pertains to where you're going to fuck me," she breathed, locking her lips over mine as she rocked her hips against me.

"Fair enough," I said with a chuckle, leading us to the bedroom.

I laid her on the king-sized bed and grabbed a condom from my wallet before tossing it on the dresser.

"There's so much I want to do with you, but right now, I just want to be buried deep inside of you," I admitted.

"We can do the other stuff later. Just fuck me now," she begged, lifting her skirt and spreading her legs to show me she wasn't wearing any panties.

"Fuck," I groaned, rushing to get out of my clothes and get sheathed in record time.

She sucked her finger into her mouth, then pulled it out and rubbed it along her slit as I watched. Her legs fell to the side, giving me an unobstructed view as she played with her clit.

"That's my job," I growled as I climbed onto the bed beside her.

"Well then, you'd better get to work."

I leaned back against the headboard and then grabbed her hand before she could make herself come, pulling her across the bed and on top of me.

"We agreed you were going to ride this cock until we both came," I reminded her. "And since you don't have any panties on, I think we should get started."

I thrust my hips up, nudging her opening with my rock-hard dick.

Her head fell back, her long, dark curls cascading down her back as she hissed in response. I nudged her again, loving the way her body was responding to me. She reached down and pulled her tank top up and over her head, then tossed it to the floor, revealing bare breasts.

"Fuck, you weren't wearing a bra either?" I groaned, my dick growing harder.

She shook her head and locked eyes with me.

"I wanted as few obstacles between us as possible," she said, lowering herself over my cock and sliding down.

I leaned my head back and shut my eyes, gripping her hips as I fought to control myself. She felt so good, it was hard not to come right then and there.

She swiveled her hips, playing around as she brushed her thumbs over her hard nipples. I reached up and grabbed her hands, pulling her closer to me as I locked my lips onto hers and deepened the kiss as I thrust up inside her.

Her legs spread slightly to allow me to slide in deeper, then she started to rock back and forth, making me crazy. I broke the kiss and lunged forward, greedily pulling a nipple into my mouth and sucking. She whimpered and grabbed a handful of my hair, yanking tightly as I continued to torture her.

She bounced harder and faster, our breathing increasing as she fucked my cock like there was no tomorrow. I lowered my hand between us and began rubbing her clit as I let her nipple pop free before capturing the other one.

Within seconds, I could feel her tighten around me as she came undone, pulling my orgasm out of me along with hers.

Fourteen

Bella

I laid in Jones' arms as he stroked my head, creating a sense of peace and tranquility I wasn't sure I had ever experienced. We had fucked like we couldn't get enough of each other, and after the third round, we were spent and needed to recuperate.

"Tell me something about yourself," I said, leaning into his side as my fingers trailed through the hair on his chest. I loved that he had the perfect amount—not too much where it felt like being with a wild animal, but just enough to remind me of how manly he was.

"What do you want to know?" he asked softly, lowering his hand to my back and pulling me into him as if we weren't already practically one person as it was.

"Something no one else knows about you."

He inhaled deeply and then let it out slowly before speaking.

"I grew up in foster care," he said slowly. "I've never had a real family and always wondered what it would be like to have one."

I turned and looked up to find sadness etched across his face.

"I'm so sorry."

He shrugged as if it were no big deal, but I could see otherwise.

"My parents were drug addicts, and when the neighbor found me, I was covered in who knows what and left by myself in the kitchen while my parents overdosed in the living room. Child protective services were called, and I entered the system when I was one."

I covered my mouth with my hand to hide the gasp that had just escaped.

"Oh my God, Jones. I can't even imagine that."

"I never knew my parents, and to this day, I don't even know if they're alive. They never tried to come for me, and by the time I was ten, I stopped hoping they would. Life in foster care wasn't perfect, and I hated going from family to family, but I knew it was better than being with parents who didn't want me. I decided then and there that I was done with them and wouldn't allow myself to ever look up what happened to them."

"I don't blame you," I said softly, hugging him tighter. "I can't imagine the pain you feel from that."

"Thanks. I stopped letting it get to me as soon as I was legally on my own. Not many people know my story, and I try to keep it that way."

"Can I ask why?" I asked.

He sighed heavily again and let his head fall back against the pillow.

"I don't want people to pity me. I had a tough childhood and a rough start in life. But I'm here, and I'm doing things on my own, even if I have a reputation for burning shit and being a terrible cook," he replied with a laugh. "If I told people that I can't cook because no one ever taught me, they would feel sorry for me, and I don't want that. But the truth is, I didn't learn many essential life skills until after I was on my own. Some of the homes I was in weren't any better than the one I was removed from. I had one home I was in the longest, and there were seven of us foster kids but never enough money to put food on the table. A lot of the time, we ate dry cereal because that's all we could find. There wasn't money for milk because our foster mom bought booze instead. There wasn't ever anyone interested enough to teach us how to take care of ourselves, so I didn't have anyone to learn from. It was a very steep learning curve once I turned eighteen and was out on my own."

"Jones, I'm so sorry," I said, trying to hide the way my voice caught in my throat.

"Don't be. I'm okay now, Bella. Nothing is going to stop me now."

He pulled the blanket around us as I shivered against him, wondering how the world could be so cruel to someone as wonderful as him. I held him close, hoping he could feel how much I already cared for him.

"Now it's your turn," he said softly.

"My turn for what?"

"To tell me something about you. What's your family like?"

I sighed heavily and snuggled closer into his chest.

"I was close to my grandparents. They were more like parents to me than my actual parents. My grandfather passed away a few years ago, and my grandma recently passed. I don't talk to my parents often, especially since I took the job with Dark Vibes. They couldn't believe their daughter would do something so *scandalous,* so we haven't spoken much since they told me about my grandma's passing."

"I'm so sorry, Bella."

"Thank you. It's okay. I feel like my life is less toxic without them in it. I miss my grandma and hate that I didn't get to say goodbye before she passed. She moved back to Italy to live with her best friend, and I was planning to visit her as soon as I could save up enough money to afford the trip. She offered to pay, but I've never liked her paying for stuff for me."

I brushed away the tear that fell, hoping Jones wouldn't notice. But then he held me tighter and kissed the top of my head as I cried in his arms.

We got up early the next morning and decided to work out together since we both had the day off. I asked him to take me by my house so I could change before we hit the trail behind his house to go for a run.

When I walked inside, I tossed my keys on the island and stopped when I spotted an envelope with a post-it note stuck to the front.

I signed for it this morning on my way out but wasn't sure if you were awake yet, or in a coma from being thoroughly fucked all night—lucky bitch. I'm not sure what this is, but it looks important, so I left it where I thought you would see it. Text me later and let me know, k?

Lia

I peeled the Post-it off and stuck it to the counter before grabbing a letter opener and tearing the envelope open. I recognized the letterhead as soon as I pulled the stack of papers out and began reading. It was from the attorney who was handling my grandmother's estate and who had helped her with things after my grandfather had passed. My parents had asked me to come over a month ago, and while I had hoped it was to discuss their change of heart over my recent career change, it had been to tell me that my Nana had died.

It wasn't the kind of loving, sit-you-down-and-break-bad-news-to-you kind of conversation you saw on TV. No, it was a sit me down and tell me that they expected I would be the one to inherit her belongings and their expectations of what I would give them if so. I was the only person she was close to and the only one who would actually mourn her passing and not be concerned with what she left me.

I quickly scanned the letter, noticing the dates he had tried to reach me. Without thinking twice, I entered his phone number and pressed send.

"Burt Barnes speaking," he answered.

"Hi, Burt. This is Bella Sanchez. I received a letter from you regarding my grandmother's estate."

"Yes, Bella, thank you for getting in touch. Unfortunately, I've had difficulty obtaining your phone number, so I apologize for the delay in reaching out. I was hoping to schedule a time to get together and discuss your grandmother's trust."

"Okay," I said nervously, chewing my lower lip. "I'm free today, but I don't know if that's enough time for you to gather everything you need."

"Today would be fine. The earlier, the better, as there are time-sensitive details we need to discuss. Can you be at my office in an hour?"

I looked down at my watch and sighed heavily.

"Yes. I'll be there."

Fifteen

Jones

"Do you want me to get you some water?" I asked as Bella sat beside me, her leg bouncing nervously on the tile floor.

She shook her head but refused to look at me while we waited for Burt to return. I didn't know much, only that Bella's grandma had passed a few months ago and that her attorney had been trying to get in touch with Bella for some time now to discuss the estate. She had barely learned about it a month ago when her parents informed her of it while trying to see what they could get from her inheritance.

I had volunteered to drive her but was surprised when she asked me to come in with her. It felt like something a boyfriend would do, but I didn't allow myself to think too hard about that and be disappointed.

"Sorry for the delay," Burt said, coming inside and closing the door behind him. He set a stack of files down on his desk and sat down. "First, I would like to extend my condolences, Bella. Margaret was a wonderful woman and admired by many in Beaumont Creek. She will be deeply missed."

"Thank you." Bella smiled, but it fell flat on her lips.

"As you may or may not know, your grandmother had a trust in place before she passed. We worked diligently to make sure everything was as she wanted it months before her dementia started to progress. As you can imagine, she was worried there would be animosity amongst the family, and petitions would be initiated to challenge whether she was of sound mind when she finalized the details. I can assure you that we have all of the documentation on file, and as hard as it may be to watch, I have a video she made to address questions about why she chose what she did."

Bella nodded as I shifted in my seat beside her.

"If you're ready, I'll go ahead and start the video."

We watched as he turned one of his monitors to face us, and a beautiful woman appeared on the screen. She looked like Bella but older, with soft wrinkles around her eyes and mouth, as if she had lived a life filled with laughter and smiles.

Burt moved the mouse and pressed play.

The woman on the screen smiled and nodded before she began speaking.

"My dearest family, if you're watching this video, then that means my time on earth has come to an end. I wish I could say this was a video to explain in detail what I've left for everyone, but it isn't. Why's that? Because I didn't leave anything to anyone except Bella.

I expect that news will be enough to clear the room, and that's fine. Bella is the only person I need to speak to anyway."

She paused for a moment and looked away while taking a deep breath and slowly letting it out.

"My sweet, Bella. You have always been the light of my life and the joy that brought a smile to my face. Even when we were separated by thousands of miles and oceans apart as I moved to Italy, I never stopped thinking about you. I am so proud of the woman you've become and that you're paving your way in a world that's not ready for someone like you. You're going to do amazing things, my love, I just know it.

But that brings me to the important part of this video—the trust and your inheritance. You know that your grandfather and I worked hard to build the life that we have. We put in the blood, sweat, and tears to build our empire and to create financial security. We did all of it together, hand in hand, as partners in life and love. Something that I want for you as well.

You also know that our family has been in a constant state of upheaval, with everyone fighting over money after your grandpa passed away. I knew then who was genuinely invested in our family and who just wanted a piece of the monetary pie.

But you, Bella, you've never asked for a single thing from me your entire life. You're the only one who came to visit your grandpa and me after he had his hip replacement. You cleaned the house and cooked meals to make sure we were okay. You spent time with us without asking for anything in exchange.

That's why it was a no-brainer decision to leave everything to you, Bella.

And while I have some terms and conditions you might not understand, I hope you can trust me. I would never do anything to hurt you, but I also know how you withdraw into yourself and refuse to let others in. I understand how much your parents hurt you, but please remember that I have always been in your corner, Bella, and want nothing but your happiness.

With that said, I have finalized the trust, and everything is yours. The money in the accounts, the stocks and bonds, all of my jewelry, the house in Beaumont Creek, the boat— everything is yours, Bella.

But there is one condition—and I know you're not going to like it."

Bella sat taller and held her breath as her grandmother paused again. I wanted to reach over and squeeze her hand, assure her that I was there for her, but I didn't want to be out of line.

"In order to claim it, you must be married by your twenty-fifth birthday. In addition, you cannot annul or terminate the marriage for at least six months. While I would love to add that you must produce a great-grandchild as well, I won't do that since I won't be here to see it. But don't worry, I'll be smiling and looking down from heaven as you hold your sweet little girl in your arms on my birthday.

I know this is all probably a big shock, and you're questioning everything you just heard. I wish I could be there to sit down and talk with you, but unfortunately, I can't. But please, sweet Bella, trust me. Trust that I would never do you wrong and have my reasons for asking this of you.

Burt will be in touch with you after I've passed, but please don't fight him on this. I love you, my Bella."

She blew a kiss, and then the screen went black as the video stopped. Burt pressed a few buttons and then turned the monitor back to face him as he gave Bella a few minutes to process everything.

"Are you okay?" I whispered, desperately needing to know.

She looked up at me with unshed tears but didn't say anything. I could see the fear and worry racing through her mind.

"I thought it would be best to hear everything from her," Burt said, clearing his throat before he began speaking again. "We'll go over the details again with the paperwork, but do you have any questions I can answer right now?"

Bella rubbed her lips together and folded her hands in her lap as she tried to gather herself.

"What happens if I don't get married before I'm 25?"

"You won't be able to take over as successor trustee and will not receive any assets."

"Who would get everything then?"

"That's hard to say. In this case, since there aren't any co-trustees and you were the sole trustee listed, any interested party could take it to court and petition to appoint a new trustee."

Bella's jaw tightened as she listened.

"I'm assuming you've been in touch with other family members already?" Bella asked quietly.

"Yes. I've been in touch with your parents as well as a few others."

"Have any of them asked about taking this to court?" she pressed.

Burt shifted uncomfortably in his chair and adjusted his tie. Bella nodded and looked at me.

"My cousin Todd has been after my grandparents' estate from the moment my grandfather passed away," she explained to me. "Shortly after he died, Todd tried to swindle his way into my grandmother's life and insisted on moving in so he could take care of her. It was just one way he attempted to manipulate her into giving him something. He thought if he could implant himself at the house, he would be entitled to the house when she died. My grandmother saw right through it and ended up having to get a restraining order to keep him away."

"Margaret knew he would come forward once he heard of her passing," Burt explained. "It's why we did everything we could to make the trust secure so things would go to you and Todd wouldn't have a way to try to claim anything."

"But I have to get married in the next three weeks," Bella confirmed with a heavy sigh, glancing at me nervously.

"Yes."

"Can't someone petition that as well?" Bella asked, leaning forward to rest her hands on the desk. "Or do I just get married and everything is perfectly fine and no problems from anyone?"

I could hear the way her voice rose an octave at the end. She was freaking out—and rightfully so. I would be, too if I just found out I was expected to get married in less than a month.

"They can," Burt said sternly. "Anyone can come forward and question the legitimacy of the marriage."

"And then what happens?"

"It would go to court."

"I can't believe this is even happening," Bella muttered, rubbing her hands down her face.

"I'm sorry. I know this is a lot to take in and process and that there's a looming deadline facing you. I wish I could have gotten in touch with you sooner. Unfortunately, it seems your grandmother had accidentally transposed two numbers in your phone number, which created some delays for me. I tried getting the correct number from your family, but they were reluctant to help after learning they weren't getting anything from the trust."

"Do my parents know that I'm…"

Burt nodded.

"And that I have to…"

He nodded again.

"Speaking as a friend of Margaret's and not an attorney, I strongly recommend getting things handled as soon as possible."

Bella looked up at him, head cocked to the side in confusion.

"What do you mean?"

"Make it official. Wear a ring. Make sure everyone in town knows about the new bride and groom. Small towns love to talk, and an upcoming wedding would be just the chatter we need right now. Nothing makes a marriage more believable than the people in town talking about it," Burt said, closing the folder he was looking at and resting his hands on top.

"Great, now I just have to find someone to marry…" Bella said, looking in a daze. I couldn't begin to imagine what she was feeling.

I swallowed hard, hating the thought that whatever was going on between us would be over just like that. Sure, we were having fun, and it was a no-strings-attached situation that Bella wanted. But now that she had to *get married,* surely this would be when she realized she could do so much better than me.

Sixteen

Bella

"You're getting *married*!" Lia shrieked, drawing attention to us as we sat around a table at Surf 'N Shack. She was on a very short lunch break, and it happened to be close to the hospital where she was doing her clinical rotations.

"Yes," I said quietly, trying to calm my racing heart. I still couldn't believe it myself. It was like I was sucked into this warped universe.

"To who?"

"I don't know." I shrugged, trying to keep the raw emotion out of my voice. Just because I was panicking and in full-blown shutdown mode didn't mean everyone needed to know about it. I looked around helplessly until I spotted Jones talking to Capshaw and Kensy at the front register. Just the sight of him and the soft smile he gave when he locked eyes with me was enough to slow my racing heart and give me a sense of peace.

He'd driven me here after we left Burt's office, though we hadn't talked about what had just happened. My head had been spinning while I fought off the urge to vomit everywhere.

"I don't get it," Lia said, leaning back and folding her arms over her chest as Jones, Capshaw, and Kensy headed our way with trays of food. "Why are you getting married if you don't even know *who* you're getting married to?"

"In order to claim the inheritance my grandmother left me in the trust, I have to be married before my 25th birthday," I explained for what felt like the hundredth time. For Lia, it had only been the first time, but I had been obsessively thinking about it since I found out.

"That's in less than three weeks." Her eyes looked like they were about to pop out of her head—s*ame, girl.*

"I know."

"So what are you going to do?" Lia asked, taking the plate of food Kensy handed to her.

I'd sent a group message, begging everyone to meet us here so I could talk to them. I could tell by the strained expression on Capshaw's face that Jones had already told him.

"I don't know. I either get married to someone in the next three weeks and inherit a bunch of stuff from my grandmother, or I don't do it, and my cousin Todd has a chance of taking what he's always wanted. I know I shouldn't say it because he's family, but I wholeheartedly hate him."

"Sounds like we're planning a wedding then," Lia said, popping a french fry into her mouth.

"You make it sound like it's so easy," I grumbled, running my hands through my hair again.

"That's because it is. Now if you told me that you had stuck a glass toy up your ass that wasn't meant to go up your ass, and we had to spend hours trying to retrieve it—that would be a problem.”

“Eww.” I scrunched my nose, even though I was appallingly curious about what they had used in the first place. “Also, having a toy stuck up your ass isn’t the same as finding out you *have to get married* in the next three weeks. I’m not in any position to be getting married!”

“You kinda are, though,” Kensy said softly, hiding behind Capshaw’s arm as she said it. “I mean, I know we’re not supposed to know that you two are doing whatever you’re doing, but we do, so there’s that. I’m just saying—you and Jones are already *dating*—if that’s what you want to call it, so why not just get married?”

My eyes felt like they were going to pop out of my head for the tenth time today. I glanced at him nervously, hating that he was likely embarrassed to be called out like this in front of our friends.

“You can’t just volunteer him to marry me,” I hissed out quietly to her.

“Sure she can,” Capshaw said, making no effort to lower his voice as he wrapped his arm around her shoulders. “Jones, do you want to marry Bella?”

The color drained from my face as I looked at him in disbelief. This time, I refused to turn to Jones, even though I could feel his gaze heavy upon me.

“I don’t know. I think the bigger question is, does she want to marry me?”

My heart fluttered wildly in my chest as he reached over and squeezed my hand.

"What do you say, Bella? Will you marry me?" he asked, getting out of his seat and kneeling on the floor as he turned me around. "I may not have a ring, but I—"

"Here you go!" Lia screeched, tossing a straw wrapper at him that had been twisted into the shape of a ring.

"Okay, I may not have a *decent* ring," he said with a laugh, grinning at the paper one in between his fingers. "But one of the first things I promise to do as your husband is to buy you a real one. Will you marry me, Bella?"

Chairs were screeching as people turned around to witness our proposal. I was still totally caught off guard by everything, but remembered what Burt said—make it official. Having everyone in town witness our proposal would only help our marriage stand up in court if it got to that point. It was now or never. This was the moment people were going to talk about.

I could either suck up my fears and accept my fake marriage to Jones, or I could deny him in front of everyone—not only embarrassing him but forfeiting my inheritance and giving Todd a chance to go after it.

I reached down and held his face in my hands as I grinned and nodded yes.

"Yes, Jones, I'll marry you!"

He stood up and placed the paper ring on my finger before lifting me to his hips as I wrapped my legs around his waist and kissed him. People cheered and applauded around us, celebrating the most romantic fake engagement they never knew they were witnessing.

<u>Seventeen</u>

Jones

"Do you want me to take you back to your place?" I asked as Bella stared out the window. "We can go back to my place, or I can take you wherever you want to go. Whatever you need, Bella."

"I have no idea what I need right now," she admitted. "I'm so sorry I dragged you into my problems, though. I appreciate you wanting to help me with this, but you really don't have to marry me."

Deciding to take charge, I turned off Main Street and headed to the place that always helped me clear my head. I knew my silence was probably killing her and creating a mountain of doubt and insecurity as she assured herself that I didn't want to marry her, but she would be wrong. I wanted nothing more than to be with Bella, and if marrying her made things easier for her, I would do it with no questions asked.

But I didn't want to have this conversation with her while I was driving. I wanted to wait until I could look her in the eyes and make sure she knew my words were true. Today had been hard enough for her already, I was going to do whatever I could to turn that around.

Ten minutes later, I put the truck in park and hopped out. I walked around and opened the door, extending my hand to help her down.

"I don't think I've ever been here before," she said, looking around at the thick forest around us. "It's gorgeous."

"Nate and Capshaw took me fishing here a while back. The lake is on the other side, but I like to come up here and clear my head when I need it. It's one of the few places that's always calm and quiet."

She stood in front of me, looking beautiful as always, with her hair pulled up on her head and the clothes she'd put on earlier to go for the run we never got around to.

"Thank you for this," she said, leaning on her tiptoes to lightly kiss my lips.

I wanted to deepen the kiss and show her how I would do anything she asked, but she didn't need me humping her leg like a dog in heat right now. She needed a friend to talk to and help her navigate the life-changing events that had been thrown at her today.

"Do you want to go for a walk?" I offered, nodding to the clearing across from us.

"That would be great, thanks. Sorry we didn't get to our run this morning."

"No need to apologize. I'm not worried about it. I was happy to be at Burt's office with you this morning."

"I still can't believe everything that happened today. I woke up this morning feeling pretty good after a night of hot sex, thinking we were going to work out and spend the day together, to finding out that I'm the sole beneficiary of my grandmother's estate. Oh, and that I have to get married in the next three weeks if I want to claim it."

She inhaled deeply and slowly let it out as we walked through the trees, the dirt crunching beneath our feet.

"It's a lot to process, and it's going to take longer than a day to sort through your feelings about it," I offered, stepping to the side and extending my hand to help her over a fallen log that was making the walkway narrower.

"How do you do that?" she asked, looking up at me as I walked beside her again.

"Do what?"

"Know all the right things to say? It's like you're in my head, and you can hear all the things I'm afraid to say, yet I don't have to say them, and you still ease my mind."

"I don't know." I shrugged. "I guess it's just a skill I learned over the years."

"Well, it's one that I'm very thankful for. You have a way of keeping me calm, and I don't even realize it most of the time. I know things between us are still really new, but in a way, I feel like I've known you forever. It's a great feeling, something I've never felt before."

"Well, I guess that's a good thing to have with someone who is your soon-to-be husband."

The moment the words left my lips, I knew it would change the vibe we had going. Bella stiffened beside me, and I could see her whole body tense up.

"Want to sit down and talk about it?" I offered, nodding to the bench coming up ahead of us.

"No," she said, shaking her head. "I'm better if I keep moving right now."

"Okay, we'll keep walking."

She nodded and locked her hands together as her fingers fidgeted anxiously. I could tell her mind was racing a mile a minute, but waited until she was ready to get the words out she needed to say. We kept on down the path until suddenly, she stopped and spun toward me. I lifted my head in surprise and reached my hand out to steady her as her eyes danced wildly, searching my face.

"It's not that I don't want to marry you, Jones," she rushed out. "I don't know if I want to get married—period. Before this morning, I didn't have to think about that. I wasn't even considering a life of being settled down and what that looked like. I've been so focused on my career and where that's taking me that the thought of marriage and a husband never crossed my mind. So please believe me that when I say this is a *me* issue—I mean it. This isn't a *you* problem. You're fantastic and wonderful, and any girl would be lucky to marry you, but I don't know if I'm that girl. What if I fuck everything up, and you're constantly disappointed in our marriage? I work strange hours, and sometimes I have to travel for work, and then there's the whole *taking my clothes off for money* thing, which sounds worse than it is—but still, you get the point. What if suddenly you're not supportive of what I do? What if my career has to stop because you don't want to be married to someone who makes money off their body? What if this ruins your life and your first wedding is a fake one, and then you los—"

"Bella," I warned softly. "Take a deep breath. Right now, breathe."

She closed her mouth and took a long, deep breath as tears filled her eyes.

"Take another breath," I coaxed, pulling her into me.

Her body was still stiff, but I held her close and wrapped my arms around her.

Within seconds, I felt her fingers grab the fabric of my t-shirt as she fell apart and cried against my chest.

"It's okay, Bella. Let it out. You're safe here with me. Fall apart and know I'm here to help put everything back together."

She cried harder, her legs starting to give out beneath her.

I picked her up and carried her to the bench, where I held her in my arms as she cried.

Eighteen
Bella

"How are you feeling?" Lia asked as she came in and set her stuff on the kitchen island. She had just gotten off from her shift at the hospital, and we hadn't had a chance to talk since I had gotten "engaged" at lunch today. Jones and I had spent most of the day together at the lake before he brought me home a few hours ago. I told him I needed some time to myself to just sit and process everything, and he assured me he was there if I needed anything. He didn't fight to stay with me, which I appreciated because I really needed some space to think.

"Good? I guess? I'm not quite sure how to answer that," I admitted. "I feel like I was just starting to be okay with my grandma passing, and then watching that video this morning made it feel like I was getting the news all over again. It was hard seeing her and knowing that she was planning for her death while I was off somewhere, chasing after my career. I should have been there with her."

"I'm sorry. I can't begin to imagine what you're going through. But I know that your grandma was so proud of you, Bella. I was there for some of your video calls with her; I saw how bright her smile was when you told her you had been selected for the Dark Vibes job. She wanted you to go after what you wanted. She was home, and that's where she wanted to be. I'm sorry you didn't get to say goodbye to her."

"I wish she was still here because I would love to know what she was thinking when she decided I had to be married by my 25th birthday in order to claim my inheritance." I shook my head, but a small smile still fell on my lips.

My grandmother was known for many things, but highly intuitive and quirky were two that always stuck out to me. She made sure I knew from an early age that it was okay to take a different path than the other kids. While they were playing outside and roughhousing, I was inside reading or learning how to cook. I've always done my own thing, and until recently, never cared what anyone thought.

"I'm sure she had her reasons," Lia offered, curling her feet beneath her. "She always did stuff that seemed weird at first, but then when she finally explained why she did, it always made sense."

"True, but this is *marriage*, Lia. Not something silly like changing all of the clocks in the house by ten minutes every day before daylight savings so you're more adjusted to the time change when it happens."

"That was actually quite genius," Lia admitted with a chuckle. "I wasn't *as* late to things as I would have normally been."

"Can we get back to the real problem here?" I whined, shifting under my blanket on the couch. It wasn't cold, but I liked the weighted comfort of it around me.

"Is it really a problem though?" Her voice was softer, so I knew she was trying to keep me calm before I escalated into a full-blown panic attack, like earlier with Jones. "Just hear me out, okay?"

I nodded and pulled the blanket tighter.

"I know the marriage part freaks you out."

"Who wouldn't be?!"

She cocked an eyebrow and waited for me to calm down again before she continued.

"Marriage is a big deal, I get it. But Bella, you're in a good position for this to be thrown in your lap right now. You're dating—even if you didn't want to admit it before now—one of the nicest guys in the world. Not only that, he adores you. Like, would do anything in the world to make you happy level of adoring you. On top of that, you're having mind-blowing sex with him, so you know, you've got the chemistry, too. These are all things that make a good marriage, and you already have them. I know you're scared of the commitment side of this, and I get it. I really do. But if you have to do this, Jones is the perfect guy to do it with. And I don't want to freak you out more than you are already, but I seriously think you guys could be destined for marriage if it wasn't already being thrown at you as a requirement of the trust."

I worried my lip between my teeth. She was right. Jones was one of the nicest people I'd ever met, and he was so selfless around me. And the sex was really great.

"But it's marriage, Lia. Legally being bound to the other person. I've never even been in a long-term relationship, and now I'm expected to just jump into a marriage. Who knows if I'll even make a good wife."

"You're going to be fine. But if you don't want to do this, you don't have to."

"But I do. Because if I don't do it, then my twerp of a cousin can petition it in court, and knowing him, he'll likely win."

"That's true, too." She nodded.

"I never wanted anything from my grandparents. I just loved that they spent time with me and gave me unconditional love. They didn't hound me about dieting after I got my first modeling gig, like my parents. They weren't concerned with using my looks to make them money. They just loved me—wholeheartedly and without expectations. They were better parents than my real parents ever were. I have my memories of them, and for me, that's enough. But it's the thought of Todd swooping in and thinking he can have something he doesn't deserve. He wasn't around when I was young unless he wanted something. They warned me about him as soon as I was old enough to understand. I hadn't seen him in at least ten years until my grandfather passed and he came looking for money. I don't want to get married right now, Lia, but even more—I don't want Todd to get a single thing of theirs. I want my grandparents to rest in peace knowing that their legacy will live on with the only person who truly loved them."

"So… does this mean…?"

"It means I'm getting married, and you and Kensy are both going to be my maids of honor."

She arched an eyebrow but dropped it when I grabbed a throw pillow and hit her with it.

"Stop it. If I have to get married, then you have to share being the maid of honor with Kensy. I love you both equally and refuse to pick one over the other."

"Fine, but I'm planning your bachelorette party." She jutted her chin up and looked at me through narrowed eyes.

"No—we're not having a bachelorette—"

"Shh. That's enough out of you. I will not have you ruin my fun planning a bachelorette party."

"You can plan Kensy's," I offered.

"She's not getting married for a while. You, on the other hand, are getting married in less than three weeks. Which means you guys need to pick a date, and I'll talk to Kensy about having your party on my next night off."

"So, like a Wednesday night thing?" I teased. "Or maybe we do Taco Tuesday and let Kensy get *crazy* with the guacamole?"

"Don't even joke about that," she warned. "You do NOT want to know what she's done with guacamole."

I shivered and shook my head.

"You're right. I don't. But really, you don't have to throw me a party. It's a fake marriage. We don't have to get all crazy about it. Jones and I will pick a date, go down to the courtho—"

"Bella," she said sternly, closing her eyes and pinching her nose between her fingers. "If you refer to this as a fake marriage again, *I'm* going to divorce you. You heard your grandmother's attorney—this needs to be as real as can be. People have to believe that you two are so in love that you decided to get married."

"Yeah, but—"

"No buts. This will work better if you stop fighting it and allow yourself to accept that you're getting married to Jones. I don't know if you're already falling in love with him or not, but I know you wear that stupid smile every time you talk about him and that you're having the best sex of your life, so I would say if you're not *in* love yet, it's just around the corner. Now, I'm going to go take a shower and try to wash off my day."

She got up and grabbed her stuff from the island before heading to her bedroom and shutting the door behind her.

While she was right about most things, I couldn't bring myself to admit that I had feelings for Jones already. It was *way* too soon to be tossing around the *l-word*, even if he was my soon-to-be husband.

Nineteen

Jones

"So, how do you feel about everything?" Capshaw asked quietly as we stocked the firetruck.

"Honestly, I don't know." I sighed heavily and looked around to make sure no one was close enough to hear our conversation.

It wasn't like the whole town hadn't heard about our engagement. Two days had passed since it happened, and that news had spread quicker than any fires I'd ever started. Hell, my locker had been decorated with balls and chains when I came in this morning. Everyone wanted to know the details of when it happened and how it happened, but I wasn't ready to talk. Not until Bella and I had a solid plan of what we would tell everyone. Our *love story* could put her inheritance at risk if we didn't get the details right and make them believable.

"Kensy was talking about having everyone over for dinner on Sunday. Are you guys up for it? I think she and Bella are getting together tonight."

"Yeah, that's what she told me earlier. I guess they were originally going to Tipsy Taquito, but since it's Friday, they decided to stay in and order takeout instead. The only one who likes the Friday night crowd is Lia, and she's working."

"It's funny how things change once you find that special someone," he replied with a smirk.

"What are you talking about?"

"Nothing." He shrugged and closed the door after we hopped down from the truck. "Just that Bella used to like getting dressed up and going out before."

"Before what?"

"You." He winked and headed inside while I stood there like a dummy, wondering if he was right.

I pulled out my phone, found Bella's name, and started a text message.

Me: Hey, how's it going?

A few seconds later, the dots started bouncing on the screen. It was just after nine in the morning, so I was hoping to catch her before she got busy.

Bella: Good, just finished working out. Getting ready to jump in the shower.

I closed my eyes and groaned. It had been days since we'd had sex, and the thought of her wet and naked in the shower sent a jolt straight to my cock.

Me: Ugh, why did you have to tell me that?

Bella: Why what's wrong?

Me: Thinking about you naked in the shower is giving me blue balls

Bella: Oh no! If you were here, I'd kiss them and make them better.

Me: If I were there, I would have my face buried in your pussy until you came on my tongue.

Bella: Shit.

Me: What?

Bella: I think I smell smoke.

Me: Really?

Bella: Yes.

Me: I'm serious, Bella. Do you smell smoke? I told you about that damn extension cord the other day. You need to get rid of it before it catches the house on fire.

I waited for what felt like an eternity for her to respond, but she didn't. My palms started sweating as my heart pounded in my chest, my thoughts racing to the worst—Bella's house was on fire. I was just about to rush into the firehouse and demand that we clear out and head over when my phone dinged with a new message. But this time, it was a picture message.

I swallowed hard as it loaded, Bella's leg spread wide with her pussy on full display as her finger pressed against her clit.

My eyes pinched shut as I tossed my head back and groaned.

"Married life getting to you already?" Rodriguez called out as he passed by, noticing my state.

"Something like that," I mumbled, though I wasn't sure if he could hear it.

Me: You are so going to pay for that when I'm off

Bella: Sounds like a threat… and I kinda like it.

Me: I was worried you were in real danger

Bella: I am. My pussy is on fire, and I need you to come put it out. Maybe some mouth-to-pussy resuscitation.

Me: And now I'm harder than a fucking Rubik's cube.

Bella: I know how to solve both—your hard cock and a Rubik's cube.

Me: Well, aren't you just filled with hidden talents?

Bella: Wouldn't you like to know?

Me: I would much rather be buried balls deep inside of your pussy, but that's not the reason for my text. I was texting you to see if you wanted to go to Capshaw's house on Sunday for dinner.

Bella: Lol, Kensy just texted me to invite us over too.

Me: Well, Capshaw beat her to it since I got the invite first.

Bella: That's debatable. Her message came through while I was taking a picture for you. I was a little distracted, or I might have seen it sooner.

Me: You're killing me.

Bella: How so?

Me: You keep talking about your pussy, and I can't think about anything else now.

Bella: Sorry. Give me a second.

I frowned as I stared at my phone, waiting to see what she was up to.

A few seconds later, another picture message popped up.

I lowered my head, debating whether anyone would believe I suddenly came down with a 24-hour bug to get out of being on shift as I stared at the picture of her perky tits and pebbled nipples, begging me to suck them. This woman was going to drive me crazy, and soon, I would be the lucky bastard who got to call her his wife.

Twenty

Bella

"Are you sure we have to go?" I groaned as I leaned my head back against the seat in Jones' truck.

"Yeah, it would be rude to cancel. But we don't have to stay long," he assured me as we headed to Kensy and Capshaw's house.

I was exhausted and sore from spending the day moving my stuff into his house. We knew it wouldn't look like a real marriage if we had separate houses, which meant we needed to move in together.

It made more sense for me to move into his house, and even as much as I hated to admit it, it felt more like home than the house I shared with Lia. It was warm and welcoming, and for some reason, it reminded me of walking into my grandparent's house—which would technically be mine if I didn't screw anything up with the trust before then.

"They're going to want to plan a wedding for us," I warned, turning in my seat to stare at him. Today was the first day I'd really seen him since he was on shift the past two days. Even though I didn't consider myself *ready* for marriage, I also wouldn't complain about having to look at his gorgeous face every day.

"Do you not want them to?" he asked, bringing me back into the present.

"I don't know." I sighed. "I hate to be so negative, but I would be fine just going to the courthouse and doing it there. The requirement says I have to be married. It doesn't say anything about me having to have a big, fancy wedding."

"True," he said cautiously. "But what if this is your only wedding? Wouldn't you want to make it special if you could?"

I felt my cheeks flush with heat. Was he saying he wanted to really marry me or that he planned to stay married to me once this was over? We hadn't talked about what would happen after the six months were up…

"What about you?" I asked, hoping to steer the focus away from me. "What kind of wedding do you want?"

He shrugged and looked at me while we stopped at a red light.

"I don't know. I've never given it much thought."

"Because you never expected some crazy girl to con you into marrying her?" I teased, hoping to make light of everything.

"No, because I never thought anyone would ever love me enough to consider marrying me."

The light turned green, our conversation over because what could I even say to that? It wasn't that I *didn't* love him, but whatever I *was* feeling was way too new for me to be able to blurt it out and possibly hurt him in the long run. He deserved better than that—better than a girl who might not make the same decision to marry him if her future wasn't on the line.

We pulled up to Kensy's house a few minutes later, neither of us bothering to speak as he helped me out. His touch was soft but felt distant as he guided me to the door with his hand on my lower back.

"Hey! I'm so glad you guys could make it!" Kensy exclaimed, holding the door and stepping back so we could enter. "I'm sorry, I didn't know you guys were getting your stuff moved today, or I would have tried planning for another day."

"It's okay. Thanks for inviting us for dinner," I said, hanging my purse on the rack behind the door.

"No problem, though I do have ulterior motives." She grinned big and rubbed her lips together as if trying to keep a secret in.

We followed her into the kitchen, where Capshaw was pulling something out of the oven. Whatever it was smelled delicious and made my mouth water, reminding me that we had skipped lunch today. Jones had insisted that we stop and eat something, but we decided to fuck instead. Priorities.

"Since Lia couldn't be here because of work, I've taken on the task of coordinating everything for the wedding," Kensy announced, grabbing a notepad and pen before walking with us to the dining room table. "We'll eat first, then get down to the details after."

"We don't have to do anything big or fan—" I started before she pinned me with a look, and I stopped.

"Lia warned me you would do this," she said with a sigh. "She also recommended that we start with this." She grabbed a bottle of wine from the shelf behind her and handed it to me. "I'll help Capshaw get dinner out if you want to help pour the wine."

I took a deep breath, already feeling my anxiety spike when I felt Jones rest his hand on my shoulder.

"Here, let me," he said, taking the bottle from my hands.

I stepped back and watched as he worked, trying not to stare too hard as the muscles in his forearm flexed as he twisted the corkscrew.

"If you keep looking at me like that, I'm going to throw you over my shoulder and haul you home," he warned, glancing over his shoulder. *Home. Our home.* Because we officially live together as of a few hours ago. Just one more change I hadn't seen coming.

"How do you know when I'm doing that?" I asked quietly, giggling.

"Because your eyes are literally undressing me right now. Capshaw is going to come out and wonder why my dick is hard from opening a bottle of wine."

"Well, it's not just any wine. It's the best of the best. It's the Chianti I used to drink with my grandmother."

"That helps," he muttered.

"What does?" I asked, confused as I leaned forward to look at him.

"Talking about your grandma. My dick isn't hard anymore."

I rolled my eyes and grabbed the wine glasses, trying to hide the grin on my face.

****

We finished dinner, and I helped Kensy clean up while the guys worked on bringing out the stuff Kensy insisted she needed from her office—which left me worried about what tonight would be like.

We sat down in the living room, and Kensy grabbed the notepad she had used to jot down a few notes on during dinner. I had expected that to be it, but apparently, we were going balls to the wall with full-on planning tonight. There were boxes spread out and lining the wall, piquing my curiosity as to what was inside them. I got comfortable and waited as the guys brought in the last one and set it with the others.

"What is all of this?" I asked, concerned when I noticed the lunatic smile on her face.

"This is us putting together your wedding. Lia and I shopped online the other night and had everything shipped here. We knew you wouldn't do this yourself and that dragging you out to a store would be useless because you would refuse to do any shopping. So, we brought the shopping to you! Plus, this is better anyway because there aren't many options in Beaumont Creek unless you want to have a nautical-themed wedding—which, if you do, I'm telling you now that I'm not coming."

I raised my eyebrows and giggled about how seriously she was taking this.

"Kensy, this is—I don't know what this is," I said nervously. "A lot of money, that's for sure. You didn't need to do all of this."

I swallowed hard, imagining the thousands of dollars they'd spent on the stuff in the boxes.

"Eh, don't worry about it," she said dismissively, waving a hand. "I have plenty in my savings from my dad's life insurance. Whatever you don't like, we'll send it back. It's not a problem at all."

It was weird seeing someone act so nonchalantly about money. I did well now, but there were plenty of times when I literally had to count my pennies just to afford food. And yet here Kensy was, buying boxes and boxes of wedding stuff to throw me and Jones the perfect fake wedding.

"So, each box contains items that match—either by color or theme—" she started, eyes widening when I held up my hand to stop her.

"Theme? No. I'm not having a themed wedding, Kens."

"Okay, okay. I get it. But just promise me you'll look at everything first, then decide. Okay?"

"Deal."

I sighed dramatically, rolling my eyes as Jones came and sat beside me.

"Alright, box number one is our tropical-themed wedding," Kensy announced as Capshaw opened the box and pulled out a short white wedding dress with a bright pink ribbon tied around the middle.

I scrunched my nose and shook my head.

"Well, okay then," she said with a laugh. "The next one we have is a Bohemian theme. The idea for this one is simplicity, which we know you like." Capshaw lifted another dress out of the next box and held it up.

It was pretty, with long, thin fabric covered with lace and a light brown sash that went with it. He pulled a flower crown out and lifted it like Simba from The Lion King but earned another frown from me.

We went through the rest of the boxes, and I was getting worried that I would hurt Kensy's feelings because I hadn't liked any of the options they'd presented to me so far. So much thought had been put into pairing the perfect items together, but nothing spoke to me. We went from beach vibes to rustic to fairytale, but nothing felt right. I'd asked for Jones to give his input a few times, but he simply kissed my hand and said it was whatever I wanted. A lot of help that was.

"Alright, our very last box. And if you don't like this one either, it's fine. I promise. We want this to be whatever you guys want," Kensy insisted before nodding for Capshaw to open the box.

"I saved this one for last because Lia and I bet on which one you would pick, and I didn't want you to not consider the other options first. But we both agree that this one is probably the most *you* that we've seen. But again, no hard feelings if you're not into it."

I inhaled deeply and held it as Jones squeezed my hand.

"We present to you the vintage theme," Capshaw said, lifting a dress out of the box that looked just like the one I had seen my grandma wear in her wedding photos.

I gasped and leaned forward, staring at it in disbelief.

"Oh my God," I whispered, turning to look at Kensy with tears in my eyes. "It looks just like—"

"It is," she said, nodding and wiping her tears away. "Jones helped us get Burt's contact information after we talked on Wednesday, so we reached out and asked him if we could have your grandmother's wedding dress. He was reluctant at first since he couldn't give you anything of hers without the requirements of the trust being met. But then Capshaw had his uncle talk to him—he's a lawyer too, and they worked it out. Thankfully, your grandma's best friend knew exactly where it was since they lived together. Apparently, your grandma had anticipated that things might *go missing* from the house here in Beaumont Creek after she passed, so she took the things she felt were most valuable with her to Italy. Her friend was so excited to share it with you and was able to expedite it for us to make sure we got it in time. It just arrived an hour before you got here. I was sweating all day, worried it wouldn't make it in time."

"I can't believe this." I stood up and walked over to Capshaw as he extended it to me. I held the dress in my hands, running my fingers over the delicate lace on the bodice. The color had changed slightly over the years, now more of a cream color. The satin of the dress was still pristine, and the lace that covered the top and created long sleeves was still in impeccable condition.

"What do you think?" I asked Jones, holding the dress against my body and moving with it.

He stood up and walked over to me, kissing me on the forehead.

"I think I can't wait to make you my wife while you're wearing that dress. It's beautiful, Bella, but nothing will ever compare to you. The more important question is, what do you think? It's your dress, and you should pick something *you* want to wear."

"I think it's fitting that I would wear my grandmother's dress to my last-minute wedding, given that this is all happening because of her," I said with a laugh.

"Then it's settled," he replied, kissing the tip of my nose. "We're having a vintage-themed wedding and already have the dress."

"Yay! She said yes to the dress!" Kensy said, pulling out her phone and holding it up for Lia to see as she FaceTimed her.

For the first time since our engagement, I reached up and kissed my fiancé in front of other people. Granted, it was just Kensy and Capshaw, but still. I could hear Lia asking questions but ignored them while I enjoyed this moment.

We spent the rest of the night planning out the small details of our wedding, and by the time we were done, we had a date, location, and guest list set. I walked out of their house with a smile on my face and feeling excited about our wedding.

Twenty-One

Jones

"I know we're living together so it makes us getting married more believable, but if you'd be more comfortable sleeping in the guest room, I can make it up for you real quick," I offered once we got home from Capshaw and Kensy's.

"We've already had sex—like *a lot* of sex," she said with a laugh. "It doesn't bother me to sleep in the same bed, but if you want your space, I don't mind taking the guest room."

My eyes narrowed as I studied her, watching the color trail up her skin as she blushed.

"I don't need space," I confirmed, stepping toward her.

"No?" Her dark eyelashes fluttered rapidly as I snaked an arm around her waist and pulled her into me.

"Nope."

"What do you need?" she asked, her own need heavy in her voice.

"I think you already know." I pressed my erection against her belly and smirked as her eyes widened.

"Well, you know, if we're doing this marriage thing, maybe we should do things the right way." Her voice was quiet, and I could tell she was having difficulty getting the words out.

"Yeah? What does that mean?"

She pressed her hand to my chest and stepped away, licking her plump lips.

"Maybe we should refrain from doing anything until our wedding night. Then consummate the marriage."

I swallowed hard, struggling past the dryness in my throat.

"You want to wait to have sex until our wedding night?" I confirmed.

She nodded, pulling her lip between her teeth as she smiled seductively at me.

My cock hardened even more, straining against the zipper of my pants.

"Okay," I said, blowing out a heavy breath. "It's only six nights. I can last that long…"

"No other stuff either," she added, turning and heading for my bedroom as she shimmied her hips, reminding me of what I couldn't have.

I threw my head back and groaned. This was going to be the longest six days *ever*.

While Bella did her nightly skincare routine, I went to the other spare room, where I had my workout stuff set up. I did a few reps of weights, then decided to run on the treadmill to burn off some extra energy, given I couldn't work it off with Bella.

Once I was done, I headed to the master bedroom and found Bella rubbing lotion onto her legs as she sat in a robe on the bed. I watched as her fingers lightly trailed up her skin, reaching the area beneath the fabric of the robe. She parted her legs slightly to rub it into her thighs, but I knew she was doing it just to torture me.

"Everything okay?" she asked, one eyebrow raised as she squirted more lotion into her hand and began working on the other leg. "You're all sweaty."

"I ran a few miles on the treadmill and lifted weights," I replied, grabbing the back of my shirt and pulling it over my head. I stepped into the walk-in closet and tossed it into the hamper before removing the rest of my clothes.

Her jaw dropped open as I walked past her to the master bathroom in all my naked glory, cock proudly saluting her on our way by.

"Jones!" she hissed, jumping off the bed and letting the bottle of lotion fall to the floor.

"What?"

"You can't just strip off your clothes and parade around here all—naked!"

"Why not?" I lifted my arm and leaned it against the bathroom door frame, knowing she was having trouble not looking down at my dick.

"Because—it's… Like… totally… Ugh. You know what?" She placed her hands on her hips and stared at me, eyes narrowing as she fumed.

"What?"

"It's inappropriate. That's what it is." She folded her arms over her chest, satisfied with her answer.

"The only reason you think it's inappropriate is because *you* decided to take a vow of celibacy until our wedding. It wasn't inappropriate when you were gagging on it while taking me deep into your throat, and you sure as hell didn't find it inappropriate when I fucked you so hard we both came twice. Don't get mad at me for being naked in my house when you're the one who decided no sex until the wedding."

She inhaled sharply, processing that.

"You know I was just kidding about the whole waiting thing, right?" she asked, shifting her weight as she allowed her eyes to drift down for a split second.

"You weren't joking," I replied, leaning forward as I lifted her chin with my finger. "And Bella?"

"Yeah?"

"My eyes are up here. I would appreciate it if you could stop ogling me like a piece of meat. I'm a man with feelings, and it would be great if you respected that before we embark upon the journey of marriage. I won't be objectified and used as a sex object," I teased, winking as I turned and gave her the perfect view of my ass as I walked into the bathroom.

I whistled an upbeat tune as I turned the water on and stepped inside. I needed the rush of cold water to cool me off before getting into bed with the most beautiful girl in the world, who I couldn't touch for six more days.

Twenty-Two

Bella

I stood there feeling completely sextrated—it's a real fucking thing when you're sexually frustrated—as Jones got in the shower and left me standing in his room, needy and aching to be touched.

Was it my fault we couldn't have sex? Yes. Did I already regret telling him I wanted to wait until our wedding night to consummate the marriage? Also, yes.

But the thing was that I kinda liked this version of Jones. I hadn't known him long enough to see this side before—but I liked it. A lot. So much so that I was tempted to get a toy and please myself while he likely jerked off in the shower because there was no way his erection was going away on its own any time soon.

I loved that he wasn't insecure about his body and didn't need me complimenting him on his big cock or rock-solid pecs. He didn't seem to even care whether I checked him out or not—though, let's be honest, we all knew I was checking him out. It was hard not to! He was sweaty, his skin glistening and begging to be touched. And even though I couldn't get a good look without getting caught staring, I was pretty sure I saw a drop of precum on the tip.

By the time he had finished in the bathroom, I had turned down my side of the bed and was changed into pajamas. IF you could call these pajamas. I couldn't tell you what possibly motivated me to pack them in my stuff when I moved things over earlier, but I was glad I did.

Jones came out, steam billowing around him, and stopped dead in his tracks as he stared at me. He hadn't bothered to put clothes on while he was in there, which made it hard *not* to stare at the bulge still lurking beneath the towel wrapped loosely around his hips.

"What are you doing?" he asked, his voice gruff.

"I was just setting some alarms for the morning," I replied, holding my phone up to show him.

The black see-through lace bra I had on shifted, pulling the fabric against my nipple, making it harder. I didn't have to check if he'd noticed it because the way he was looking at me said he noticed everything.

"What are you wearing," he clarified, gripping the towel tighter.

"Oh, this?" I looked down as if I hadn't already seen the ensemble. "This is what I sleep in at night."

"A lacy thong and matching bra?"

"Mmhmm."

"That's funny. I don't remember you wearing anything like that during the nights we've spent together."

"Oh… um. Yeah. I just, you know, really like this one," I lied, hearing the change in my voice again. "Does it bother you? I don't want to make things *hard* on you, so I can change if you need me to."

"Nope. Not at all. I'm fine." He grabbed the towel and pulled it from his waist, revealing his glorious cock again. "Just as long as you're okay knowing I sleep naked."

He tossed it to the floor and climbed into bed beside me.

I slid down under the covers and set my phone on the charger as I wondered how I was going to make it six nights sleeping next to this *beast* without touching it.

"Good night, sleep tight," he said, rolling over to face me.

"Not as tight as my vagina," I muttered, rolling away from him so I didn't risk giving in and jumping his bones.

The next morning, I woke up to a familiar stiffness pressing into my butt. I smiled and shifted against it, wondering if Jones had realized his arm was wrapped over my body or that his cock was lined up perfectly at my entrance.

I pretended to be asleep as I moved as slowly as possible, lining it up even further.

Firm hands gripped my hips, stopping me.

"Don't even think about it," he murmured, sleep still heavy in his voice.

"How do you always know?" I groaned, throwing my arm over my head.

"I know more about you than you think. And while I would love nothing more than to plow my cock inside your wet pussy, we both know that's not going to happen."

"Well, it's not my fault you decided to invade my space and cuddle me in your sleep," I countered. "I was doing just fine without your erection against my ass this morning."

"Actually, you weren't," he said, rolling onto his back and turning his head to look at me. "I was holding you because you were crying in your sleep, and I didn't want you to feel alone. I've been holding you for about forty-five minutes."

"What?" I asked in disbelief, rolling over to see his face better.

He nodded and rolled onto his side.

"You were talking, but I couldn't make out the words. Then you started crying, and I couldn't stand the thought of you crying in your sleep, so I held you. After a little while, you stopped crying and seemed like you were having peaceful dreams, but then you started crying again."

I rubbed my hands down my face, embarrassed this had happened.

"But—your dick was hard," I blurted out a few minutes later. "If you were just holding me while I cried in my sleep, why did you get an erection?"

He chuckled and shook his head.

"Bella, you're wearing a see-through lace thong with your ass on full display, and it's morning—how could I not have an erection?"

I covered my mouth and giggled, but everything stopped being funny when he threw the blankets back, climbed out of bed, and walked naked into the bathroom. Living with a naked Jones was going to be hell for six days.

<u>Twenty-Three</u>

Jones

I thought about cooking naked so Bella had something fun to walk out to once she finished showering and getting ready. But I wasn't sure who that would hurt more—her or me.

It wasn't that I didn't respect Bella wanting to wait to have sex until we were officially married, but I was pretty sure you couldn't un-consummate what we had already done. Being in bed next to Bella wearing the lingerie set she had on last night was pure torture. It took everything I had not to rip it off of her and make love to her in our bed.

It still felt weird to say *our bed*, but I couldn't complain about sharing it with someone like her. I wanted to believe that this was how our relationship would have normally progressed if we hadn't been forced into getting married this weekend. Now, there was no way to know for sure, but I was determined to do whatever I could to make things work with Bella. Both for the fake marriage and because I was actually starting to fall for her.

Not that I could ever tell her that because I didn't want to scare her or create worry if she didn't feel the same way. But I also couldn't deny the emotions that constantly consumed my every thought because they were so different than anything I'd ever experienced before.

I was flipping the bacon in the skillet when Bella walked in.

"Perfect timing," I said, glancing over my shoulder. "Breakfast will be ready in a few minutes."

"Thank you, but you didn't have to cook for me. I usually just do one of my smoothies."

"It's already made and by the Keurig. I'm making spinach and egg white omelets, as well as turkey bacon. Wasn't sure what you might like, but it will be ready in a few minutes."

"Can I help with anything?" she asked, standing beside me, looking up under thick, dark lashes.

A flashback of admiring her same features as she sucked my cock popped into my head, causing me to get distracted as a splatter of grease popped and burned my hand.

"Shit," I cursed, pulling it away quickly.

"Are you okay?" She reached for my hand to check it, but I focused on the stove instead. We were lucky I had gotten this far with cooking without burning the house down; no need to tempt the universe.

"I'm fine, thank you. This is one of the few meals I can usually make without catching anything on fire," I explained, turning the burner off and setting the hot pan on one of the back burners.

"Are you sure? I can get some ice or something," she offered.

"Nah, I'm okay. Really. I burn myself all the time while cooking. Usually, bacon doesn't startle me that easy, but I was distracted."

A faint blush crept up her cheeks.

"Also, just because I eat this doesn't mean it's edible. You don't have to eat it if you don't want to. Also, your smoothie seemed pretty self-explanatory, so I hope I didn't screw that up."

"I'm sure everything is perfect." She smiled at me as she reached into the cabinet and took out some plates.

I was surprised when she grabbed an omelet and some bacon for herself, but the pride radiated off my face as she took a bite and didn't immediately cringe. Instead, her eyes widened as if she couldn't believe it tasted good and was pleasantly surprised.

I cut a piece with my fork and took a bite, relieved that it was how it usually tasted. It wasn't like I grew up with gourmet food, so I didn't have high expectations of what it should taste like. But then again, my basis for comparison had always been stale cereal, so it wasn't like I knew what others considered good food either.

"This is really good, thank you," she said, wiping her mouth with a napkin as she chewed.

"You're welcome. I'm glad you like it."

"So, what's on your agenda for today?" she asked, taking a drink.

"I'm going shopping with Capshaw this morning, and then he wanted to check out some options for the bachelor party he insists on throwing. You?"

"I have a photo shoot this morning with Kensy, and then we're going shopping too."

"For wedding stuff?"

She shook her head, another adorable blush kissing her skin.

"Do I want to know?" I asked, my voice straining against my throat as my mind ran wild with ideas.

"Well, she thought I might need something for the wedding night."

"Like a new outfit to tease me with?" I raised an eyebrow as I waited.

"Maybe." She giggled and took another bite, letting the fork sit between her lips longer than necessary before she pulled it out.

"You're gonna be the death of me," I muttered, shaking my head.

"Well then, I guess I shouldn't tell you that my photoshoot this morning involves some super risqué lingerie, should I?"

Heat rushed through me as I thought about Bella wearing something sexy like the lingerie she tried to pass off as pajamas last night. My dick stirred, getting the message loud and clear as I pictured her lying on a bed, hair spread out around her as she puckered her lips that looked so good wrapped around my cock. A come hither look in her eyes as she chewed her lower lip and teased me.

"Hey, Jones?"

"Yeah?" My eyes shot up to hers, embarrassment washing over me from getting caught.

Her grin spread wide across her face.

"What did you say your favorite color was?"

"Red."

"Perfect. Thank you, and thanks again for breakfast."

She got up, cleared her plate, and then left the kitchen while I sat there, picturing all the ways she was going to drive me out of my mind.

Twenty-Four

Bella

"I'm almost ready," I called out to Kensy as I struggled to get the corset up over my boobs. "The girls don't want to behave today."

"Need some help?" she offered.

"I think I got it. But remind me that I'm wearing crotchless panties so I don't just flash my vag at you. No one needs that kind of unexpected greeting."

"Noted." She laughed, making my nerves dissipate some.

I tugged at the top, getting everything aligned, then stepped into the bedroom where we were doing the photos.

"Okay, I'm ready," I said shakily.

Kensy was sitting at her desk and turned around, her eyes widening as she took me in.

"Is it too much?" I asked nervously, ready to rush out and change into something else. This campaign was meant to be more risqué than the others, but I had been assured that I didn't need to do anything outside my comfort level. I was pleased they still allowed me to work with Kensy and didn't demand I go to a studio of their choice. But I guess there was a different set of rules when it came to working as a model for a sex toy company. And I had quickly learned that the owner of Dark Vibes, Elliott Weston, didn't give a fuck about rules unless he was making them.

"No. Not too much at all." She grinned and nodded her head. "These are going to be so hot, Bella. I can't wait to see them. Did you decide which toy you want to use to cover your lady bits for those shots?" she asked as she picked up the camera and pointed it at me to check the settings.

"I was thinking about using the one with the piercing. It seems more fitting, especially since they're promoting it with this outfit," I replied, looking down at the tight red leather and lace combo that wrapped tightly around my skin.

"Sounds good. We can definitely make that one work. It's big, so we don't have to get too creative with angles. I can do enough to make sure it's clear that you're wearing crotchless panties without showing anything else."

"Perfect." I climbed onto the bed, making sure my red leather stiletto heels didn't snag the bedding. "Maybe I'll make use of the toy tonight so I can get rid of some of this stupid built-up tension," I grumbled.

"Why not just have Jones help?"

"I made the stupid decision to hold off on sex until our wedding night so we could consummate the marriage," I explained, getting in the position I always started with.

I sat with my spine straight, boobs pushed forward, stomach sucked in, and legs bent perfectly beside me as Kensy moved around, trying to find the right angle she wanted to start with.

"Haven't you guys already had sex?" She stopped and looked at me, confused.

"We have. Lots of it. Really great mind-blowing-best-of-my-life-I-would-sell-an-organ-to-do-it-again sex."

"And you decided now was the time to put the brakes on that?" She raised her eyebrows and held her camera at her side.

"Yes, because I'm stupid and don't know what I was thinking. I guess it just felt like something fun we could do to make it feel like a real wedding." I shrugged. "Or maybe I just wanted to be in control of something since it feels like everything else is out of my control right now."

"I get that. I can see how it feels like everything is being forced upon you, especially with having to get married before your birthday. But Bella, you still have so much control in all of it. You get to pick who you marry. What day you get married. What dress to wear. Where to have it. There's a lot you're getting to decide here, but I understand how you must be feeling with all of it happening at once."

"Thank you. I really needed to hear that."

Kensy smiled and then began taking pictures. We'd worked together for so long that we didn't need to talk much about what poses we were aiming for or what she needed me to do. It was a process we had perfected because it worked.

"Have you given any thought to inviting your parents?" she asked quietly with the camera still lifted to her face.

"I'm not going to."

She lowered it and gave me a soft smile.

"I know you're mad at them right now, but don't you think it might make it more real if they were there? Won't people question why they aren't?"

"I've thought about that," I admitted, changing positions so I was on my knees with my hands braced against the wall, fingers splayed with my knees spread apart. "But I think if they're there, it'll make a bigger mess out of everything. If anything, they'll be the ones who question if it's legitimate. I don't need that stress, you know?"

"I do," she replied softly. "I totally get it."

We kept working, changing the conversation to her and Capshaw so I could have a break from talking about my parents and the upcoming wedding. Finally, we finished the last outfit change and got the shots we needed with the new toys they were getting ready to launch. I climbed off the bed and headed to change when Kensy stopped me.

"Hey, I know we haven't talked about it, but I have a crazy idea," she said, scrunching her face as she smiled.

"I'm already scared," I admitted.

"Don't be. It'll be fun, I promise."

"Is it something like throwing darts while blindfolded?"

"No." She shook her head after taking a second to consider it. "No, it's nothing like that. I was thinking since you're already here and we're doing photos anyway, what about doing a few boudoir photos for Jones? It can be an early wedding present. I can have them edited and printed for you to give him the night before."

"I don't know," I replied, my head moving back and forth.

"Why not? He's already seen you naked, and I've seen the way he looks at you, Bella. He wouldn't mind having some photos to check out with you looking all sexy in them."

"Isn't that weird, though?"

"Why would it be weird? I do a lot of boudoir sessions across the board. Some are already married, some are engaged, some are just dating, and others do them for themselves. There's nothing wrong with taking sexy pictures and looking back on them over the years."

"I know, but it just feels like an odd thing to do because this is a fak—"

"If you dare say the word *fake* again, I'm gonna stuff a dirty sock in your mouth," she warned, eyebrows raised.

"Eew. Gross."

"Don't make me do it, Bella. I will. I'll go dig Capshaw's socks out of the hamper from his run this morning. You do NOT want to smell those."

"I love it when you talk dirty to me," I teased, winking at her. "Nothing says *sexy photos* like talk of dirty, smelly socks."

She rolled her eyes, but the corners of her lips still quirked up.

"So, do you want to do these or not?"

"Do I have a choice?" I asked.

"No. Not really."

Now it was my turn to roll my eyes.

"I didn't bring anything special for this, and I can tell you that if I take pictures with the pierced toy, he's going to lose his mind. He hates that toy."

"Don't worry about that. I have this covered. I might have asked Capshaw to bring a few things home in anticipation of this." She winked, which had me even more worried.

My brow furrowed as I studied her.

"What do you mean you *have this covered*?" I pressed, frowning harder when she set her camera down and rushed out of the room. "Kensy?" I called after her. "What do you mean you have this covered?"

Twenty-Five
Bella

"Are you sure we should start with this one?" I asked nervously, wearing the same red leather lingerie set we started with—the one with the crotchless panties.

"Yes. It'll be perfect, and you said his favorite color is red, so it's double perfect."

I climbed onto the bed and followed her lead as she put me in the position she wanted. I was finally starting to relax a little, reminding myself that I take these kinds of pictures all the time for work. But the problem was that these weren't for work, they were for the man who I was still getting to know and would be marrying this weekend.

We started with some basic poses, probably her way of easing me into this. I sat on the bed with my back to her as I looked over my shoulder. My hair was down, the dark curls tickling my back where the thin straps of fabric held the panties in place. Then she had me lay down, angling my legs so that I wasn't exposed. I sighed softly, settling in to the experience once I realized it wasn't any different than what I did for Dark Vibes. We kept going, working our way through the routine we'd gotten so accustomed to.

"Okay, now carefully stand up, press your hands against the wall like we did earlier, and spread your legs," she directed.

I did as she asked and was lost in thought as she moved around me. Suddenly, she stopped and gasped when she crouched down to get the angle we usually get, both of us suddenly forgetting about the crotchless panties.

"Oh my God!" She pinched her eyes closed while the camera stayed aimed at my vagina.

"Sorry!" I shrieked, rushing to cover myself up.

"No! Don't move," she commanded, holding her hand up for me to stop as her eyes fluttered open, looking anywhere but *there*.

I gave her a questioning look, but I could see the wheels turning in her head.

"Do you trust me?" she asked.

"Usually."

"Okay, hear me out—these aren't going to be for anyone but Jones, right?"

I nodded.

"And you know I don't share access to your photos with anyone. It's in our contract."

"Yes."

"I know I'm already pushing your limits," she said cautiously. "BUT, what if we gave him something to really look at?" She wiggled her eyebrows suggestively.

I'd done boudoir shoots with Kensy before I started my assignment with Dark Vibes, but they were always tasteful and tame for her to use to build her portfolio. This would be something new for both of us.

"Kensy! You can't be serious."

"Why not? It's no different than him sending you a dick pic or you sending him a flap snap." She shrugged like this was the most normal conversation in the world to be having right now.

"A what?" My eyebrows rose higher on my forehead.

"A flap snap. Clam cam. Beaver teaser. Whatever you want to call it."

"I don't want to call it any of that. My beaver won't be teasing anyone, thank you very much."

"Umm, hate to break it to you, but it already is with this whole vow of celibacy."

"It's for like SIX DAYS," I groaned. "It's not that big of a tease. I'm the one hurting the most in all of this."

"Unless you give him something to tease him until the wedding night," she said with a sly grin.

"I don't know," I said with a sigh as I tossed my head back. "Is this even something guys want?"

"Oh yeah. They want it. If they could only pick one sexy picture of you, they'd go with a beaver teaser. Hands down."

"How do you know this?" I didn't really want to know the answer but asked it anyway.

"Well, let's just say Capshaw has an entire album of them, and it's the number one pose I get requested with boudoir sessions."

"Ugh, why do I have the feeling I'm going to regret this?" I groaned.

"Because you are."

I cocked my head to the side and glared at her.

"Not in that way. You're going to regret this because as soon as he sees that picture, he's going to be a walking-talking hard on until the wedding night. Just wait and see. You'll think everything is fine, then suddenly a vase gets knocked over because he's constantly sticking out and—"

"Okay, I get it," I said, holding my hand up to stop me. "I can't believe the things I let you talk me into."

"Don't worry, I have something that will make it better." She rubbed her lips together and then left the room. A few minutes later, she returned with a bottle of wine.

"If you're suggesting I use that to—"

"Eew, no," she shrieked. "It's for liquid courage."

She plucked the cork out and handed me the bottle we had opened last night. I took a big swig and then used the tissue she handed me to blot my lips so I didn't smear my lipstick.

"Stay in the position you're in, and I'm going to come under you—"

"What?!"

"Not like *come* come. But, like, slide in beneath you."

"I'm sexually frustrated, Kens. You're not making that any better."

"I swear, I'm not trying to sound dirty! Here, have another drink."

She handed me the bottle again, and this time I poured some into my mouth without letting it touch my lips.

"Shit. I think I need some, too."

She took it back from me, lifted it to her lips, and took a big swig before sitting it on her desk.

"Okay, are you ready?"

"As ready as I'll ever be. My legs are starting to shake from holding this position for so long."

"Sorry, I'll try to get in and out as quickly as possible."

I sucked in a deep breath and slowly exhaled as Kensy climbed beneath me while I tried to refrain from bursting into a fit of laughter.

"Jesus, it's really tight in here," she mumbled, wiggling to squeeze herself in between my legs. I could spread them further, but she was already making the bed feel wobbly, and I didn't trust myself to move in the stilettos I still had on.

I looked down at her and pinned her with a look.

"Right. Sorry. No more commentary from me."

I pressed my tongue to the top of my mouth and started counting to 100 as I tried to distract myself from having her face so close to my exposed pussy.

"Alright, I'm going to take a few close-ups since you've gone through the effort of waxing. Then I'm going to zoom out and do a full-body one if I can. We might have to change positions for that one."

I nodded and did as she asked while we worked on getting the photos she wanted. A few minutes later, she climbed off the bed with me trailing after.

"I'm so happy you agreed to do these," she said with a big smile as she set her camera down on the desk. "Did you want to see what Capshaw brought home? We still have plenty of time to do a few firefighter ones."

"Sure. What all do you have?" I was fully committed now, beaver teaser and all, so there was no point in being shy now. If I was going to give these to Jones, it might be fun to see his reaction to me wearing some of his gear.

She walked over and grabbed a bag from the closet.

"He didn't have much, but I thought we could do a few of you wearing the helmet—but I want to save that for last because I thought it would look cool if we sprayed some water and I don't want to ruin your hair or makeup until we're almost done. We also have a pair of turnout pants and suspenders. I thought this would look super sexy with that black lace bodysuit that makes your boobs look amazing. Shit, I should have asked you to bring that one with you when we were talking last night."

"Luckily for you, I planned ahead and brought it. Though I thought I would be using it for Dark Vibes, it seems fate had other plans I wasn't aware of," I teased.

We spent a few hours getting the rest of the photos done, which left me excited for Jones to see them. I wasn't sure if it was the wine we had been drinking or if maybe I was just having a sudden change of heart about things. Either way, I couldn't wait to see him later, and that was a feeling I didn't want to get rid of.

Twenty-Six

Jones

"Do we have to have a bachelor party?" I asked as Capshaw drove down Main Street as we headed to the firehouse to drop off the stuff we'd picked up for Kensy and Bella.

When Capshaw proposed getting married at the station, my immediate reaction was to say no and give Bella whatever wedding she wanted, wherever she wanted. But then her face lit up, and she started planning out the small details with Kensy, and I couldn't object if I wanted to. Her happiness was all that mattered to me, and if getting married there was good enough for her, it was good enough for me, too.

In all honesty, it always felt like home for me there, and even though they weren't my *real family*, they felt more like family than anyone ever had in my life. Getting married with my *family* and friends there to witness it was something I never thought would happen.

"Yes, we have to have one," he said, gripping the steering wheel as he turned into the parking lot. We got out, loaded up as many bags as we could carry, and headed inside.

"My parents are watching Brayleigh for me all weekend, starting Friday night, so I can be the *best* best man there is. That means *I* am officially off daddy duty as of Friday morning, so suck it up, Buttercup. You're having a fucking party."

He nudged me with his elbow as we set the stuff down beside the pile of other bags and boxes that had been lined up in the kitchen.

"First, does that mean *I* can't call you daddy this weekend?" Kensy asked, coming up behind him and wrapping her arms around his waist. "And second, what kind of fucking party are you having?"

Bella shook her head and laughed as she stepped out of the way and stood beside me.

"You can always call me daddy," he murmured in her ear but not low enough to spare the rest of us from hearing it. "And Jones is just getting a bachelor party—zero fucking involved. You, on the other hand, can have a special party Saturday night if you're a good girl."

I blew out a breath and turned to Bella, hoping to ignore what was happening beside us.

"So, how did your photoshoot go?" I asked, leaning against the wall.

Her eyes widened as a rush of color filled her cheeks.

"Tell him about it, Bella," Kensy coaxed, watching us over Capshaw's shoulder as she wrapped her arms around his neck.

"It was fine," Bella rushed out quickly. "Just the usual, run-of-the-mill, everyday kind of photos. No big deal."

My eyebrows rose almost as high as her voice.

"Oh really?"

She bobbed her head and looked around, not allowing herself to look me in the eye.

"What kind of photos did you take?" I pressed, stepping closer to her as my curiosity grew stronger. I'd long admired Bella for her positive body attitude and not being afraid to show it off with the modeling work she did, so this reaction from her intrigued me.

"None," she lied, her cheeks getting redder. "I mean, you know, just the usual standard work ones. Boring, dull, work photos." She shrugged and took a step back, nearly tripping over a bag at her feet.

I reached over and grabbed it as it almost toppled over, surprised to see my helmet sitting on top.

I slowly took it out, examining it in front of her as she squirmed, nervously chewing her nail.

"So, um, why do you have my helmet?" I asked, holding it up in front of her.

She went to answer but then stopped. The red lipstick looked like it was going to smear from the amount of times she rubbed her lips together.

Enjoying this a little too much, I squatted and set the helmet down before reaching into the bag and pulling out a pair of turnout pants and suspenders.

"Is there something I should know?" I asked, looking up at her, one eyebrow arched as the fabric hung in my hand.

She shook her head but refused to say anything.

"Did you use them?" Capshaw asked Kensy, pulling my attention to them. They had finally separated, even though she was still tucked into his side with his arm wrapped protectively around her shoulder.

Kensy nodded but couldn't keep the ear-to-ear grin from spreading across her cheeks.

"They were soooo hot," she whispered, again, loud enough for everyone to hear.

Bella turned away from everyone and covered her head with her hands.

"You knew about this?" I asked Capshaw, tossing the stuff back into the bag.

"I know about everything."

"Good, you can deal with that while I deal with this," I said, standing and shoving the bag into his hands before grabbing Bella's hand and dragging her through the station.

She giggled and held on tightly as we rushed through the building, a few guys nodding in greeting along the way. I knew all of them, even though they weren't in my platoon, but I wasn't willing to stop and make any introductions right now.

I pushed through a set of double doors that led to the back office that was never used. I closed the door, startling Bella as it slammed shut. I didn't bother turning on the lights because I knew she was already feeling shy around me. Instead, I gently pushed her against the door and pinned her there with my body against hers.

She shuddered beneath my touch, and I craved to feel more, to be inside of her. But now wasn't the time or place for that. Besides, she had made a vow of celibacy, and I was going to make sure we stuck to it.

"What kind of photos did you take with my gear, Bella," I asked, my teeth barely grazing the shell of her ear.

Her head fell to the side, allowing me access to her neck.

"I'm not telling," she whispered, grabbing my shirt to pull me closer.

"Like hell you're not." I nudged her head further to the side with mine before placing open-mouthed kisses down her throat and across her collarbone.

She whimpered softly, her legs parting as my erection pressed against her stomach. I reached down and lifted her to my hips, still pinning her to the wall as I gripped her ass and held her steady.

"Tell me, Bella."

"It's a surprise. You're gonna have to wait."

"I'm not very good at waiting so why don't you tell me, and then I'll be surprised when I see them?"

"Who says I'm going to let you see them?" Her voice was flirty, teasing me in the best way.

"Well, I guess I'll just have to give you a good reason to show me." I pressed myself harder against her now that her pussy was lined up with my cock.

She gasped, her nails digging into my shoulders.

"Jones," she whimpered.

"I can make you come real good without even touching you, baby. You can keep that vow of celibacy, and we can both get what we want. But first, you have to tell me what kind of photos you took with my gear."

She closed her eyes and began rocking herself against me. I didn't want her to come just yet, so I held her hips to stop her.

"Tell me," I growled as her eyes fluttered open.

She sighed heavily, ready to give up, but I wasn't having it.

"Look, Bella, we both know you're already wet and ready for me. We also know that we're not having sex for *six more nights*. But there's no need for you to be frustrated when I can take care of your needs right now. I can give you the release you need; I'm just asking for one little thing in return."

"Fine," she said, blowing out a frustrated breath. "But I need my phone for this."

I frowned as I pulled back enough for her to reach into her pocket to pull it out. She slid her finger across the screen to unlock it, then turned it to face me a few seconds later.

My heart began to race as I stared at the picture of Bella wearing my turnout pants and suspenders with a black lace bodysuit-looking thing underneath. I had no idea what it was called, but my dick grew harder at the lowcut, plunging neckline that showed her plump, full breasts in all of their glory. The fabric was sheer, showing enough of her nipples while still leaving some to the imagination.

She grinned as she pulled her phone away and tucked it back into her pocket.

"Happy?" she asked, resting her arms around my neck.

"I'm going to see how much it costs to buy a set to keep at home. We're fucking playing firefighter as soon as we say I do, Bella. I don't care who's there, I don't give a fuck about cutting cake or tossing garters. I want to chase your sweet pussy up a tree and rescue her."

"Mmm," she moaned, closing her eyes as I rubbed my cock against her.

"I wish I could touch you to feel how fucking wet you are right now."

I rocked harder against her, working to find the perfect position to stimulate her clit. It was challenging with clothes on, but I respected her wishes and wasn't going to try to manipulate her to get around them. We were both horny and sexually frustrated, but at least I could take care of her now and then deal with mine later in the privacy of my own home.

"After we say our vows and finish all the legal stuff, I'm going to toss you over my shoulder and bring you right back to this room, where I'll sit you on that desk and eat your pussy."

She moaned louder, getting closer. I knew the dirty talk was getting to her as much as it was me.

"Then, after I've finished, I'm going to hike your wedding dress up and fuck you from behind the way you like it, Bella. I'm gonna pound your pussy so hard you won't be able to take all of my cock. When I'm done, you'll be ruined for any other man. No other cock will ever be good enough."

"Yes, Jones!" she cried out, nails digging hard into my skin through the fabric of my shirt.

"God, Bella, when I can finally come inside you, you're going to be dripping my cum for days. It'll be running down your legs, unstoppable, letting every man know you're mine. That I've marked you."

Her breathing grew quicker, and I knew she was right on the brink. I pressed harder where she needed and began to thrust against her clit, giving her the friction to send her over the edge.

"This pussy is mine, Bella. I lick it. I eat it. I fuck it. I will own it as of Saturday. No one else will ever touch it again, baby. Not even you."

I felt her squeeze my waist as her legs tightened around me as she came undone. Her head fell back while she tried to calm her breathing, giving me the perfect opportunity to kiss her neck the way I knew she liked.

When it came to Bella, her happiness was mine, and I would do whatever it took to give it to her.

Twenty-Seven

Bella

"We're all finished up here. Do you guys want to grab some dinner?" Kensy asked, holding Capshaw's hand as Jones and I joined them in the kitchen.

I felt her curious eyes on me as she likely noticed the flush of color on my face or that my hair was likely a mess from being rubbed against the door.

"Umm, what do you want to do?" I asked Jones, turning to look at him.

"Dinner sounds good to me if you want to go."

I smiled, forgetting for a second that Kensy was still waiting for my answer as I stared up at his handsome face, taking in his features.

"Ahem," Kensy said, clearing her throat.

"Oh, right," I giggled, turning back to them. "Sure, sounds great. Where do you guys want to go?"

Kensy looked at Capshaw and then back at us.

"I feel like I should suggest someplace fancy that we never go to, but—"

"You really want tacos and guacamole, so you want to go to Tipsy Taquito instead?" I offered.

"God, are we that predictable?" She covered her face with her hands.

"Yes, but it's adorable," I assured her, following them outside and getting into Jones' truck.

Tipsy Taquito wasn't as busy on Monday nights as the rest of the week, likely because everyone gravitated to the pub on the other side of town that had a Monday night special on wings and beer. We placed our orders and then grabbed a booth toward the back.

"So, have you guys thought about where you want to go for your honeymoon?" Capshaw asked before popping a tortilla chip into his mouth.

"Oh, ummm…" I stammered, not sure how to answer that because we hadn't discussed it yet. We had been so focused on getting the wedding situated that I hadn't even thought about what came after.

"We haven't talked about it yet," Jones answered for me.

"You'll need to go to Italy at some point to collect your grandmother's things, right?" Kensy asked, leaning forward against the table.

"Yeah, but I won't have access to anything until after we've been married for six months."

"Well, I don't want to plan everything for you," Kensy said nervously, looking at Capshaw. "But what if you did your honeymoon in Italy? It would be so romantic, and you'd be there anyway for your grandma's stuff. You could plan it for right after the six-month mark."

"That's true, but I don't want to cheat Jones if he had something else in mind for after the wedding."

I turned to him only to find the cutest smile on his face as he looked back at me.

"You already know my plans for right after the wedding, Bella. Anything after that is whatever you want."

A smirk crossed his face as he challenged me, my skin flushing quickly in response.

"Well, it looks like we are wide open," I said awkwardly, turning back to face Kensy and Capshaw.

Jones leaned in, his breath hot on my ear as he reached for a chip from the bowl. "Just like your legs will be," he said, low enough that only I could hear.

Kensy started talking about her ideas for possible local trips we could take in addition to a delayed honeymoon in Italy, but I was too distracted by Jones's fingers as they brushed against my thigh under the booth.

I got up and excused myself as I headed to the bathroom to compose myself. This man was going to make my mind mush before we even had a chance to get married. I stood in front of the sink, studying myself in the mirror, thankful that no one else was in there so I could have just a few minutes to myself.

I was thankful to have such good friends in my life to help me through all of this, as well as one of the nicest guys in the world who was agreeing to marry me for all the wrong reasons. But on top of that, I finally felt like I was coming into my own skin. My parents may not have approved of what I was doing career-wise, but that didn't matter anymore. After seeing Jones' reaction to the photo earlier and the way his grip on me tightened as his desire spiked—that made me feel on top of the world and unstoppable.

Knowing that I had already spent too much time in the bathroom for the others not to get concerned, I splashed some water on my cheeks and then patted them dry with a paper towel. Maybe a cold shower when I got home would help.

I opened the door and started down the hall when a guy standing off to the side startled me.

"You're that girl from the lingerie photos, aren't you?" he asked, pushing off the wall and coming into the light.

His green eyes gave me chills as they roamed over my body as if trying to confirm it was me.

"Excuse me, I'm trying to get past," I said, putting as much assertiveness in my voice as I could muster. I was used to blowing guys off, but something was different about him, and I felt this sudden urge to panic.

I tried to step around him, but he moved first, blocking my path.

"You are. You're Bella Sanchez."

My blood ran cold as I stared into his eyes, chills spreading over my skin.

"I need to get going. My fiance is waiting for me." I raised my voice but knew it was pointless; we were too far away for anyone to hear.

"I really love your work," he continued, ignoring my request to leave. "Dark Vibes is lucky to have such a beautiful girl in their catalog. I especially liked the full-page spread of you with the waterproof vibrator in the tub. Even through the bubbles, I could still see your nipples when I zoomed in enough. That's why it's important to have a good photographer. The quality is always superb with your photos."

"Look, you're making me uncomfortable," I said sternly. "Move out of my way. Now."

"Sorry," he said, holding up his hands as he laughed. "Just wanted you to meet one of your biggest fans."

I rolled my eyes as I pushed past him, desperate to escape.

"Oh, and Bella?"

I didn't want to stop or give him the time of day. I just wanted to get back to Jones and forget I ever met this creep. But something deep inside told me to turn around.

"If I were you, I'd be careful where you go running. Not all places around town have the best lighting, and I wouldn't want you to run into any trouble."

I stood there stunned as he walked past me and disappeared.

Twenty-Eight

Jones

"What's wrong?" I asked, immediately noticing the panicked look on Bella's face as she scooted into the booth beside me.

She shook her head, eyelashes fluttering as she blinked rapidly.

"There was this guy who stopped me as I was coming out of the bathroom," she said, still flustered. Capshaw and Kensy stopped talking, all eyes on Bella.

"Are you okay?" Kensy asked, reaching her hand over to touch Bella's arm.

"Yeah? No? I don't know." She shrugged and then looked at me. "He told me I should be careful where I go running. He recognized me from my modeling stuff. Knew that I was working with Dark Vibes. He knew so much about me…"

Her voice trailed off as my temper skyrocketed.

"What did he look like?" I asked, my voice tight as I searched the room.

"He was tall and thin, maybe 5'8 or 5'9. Short blonde hair and green eyes that gave me the creeps. They were super dark, almost like the forest green color of his t-shirt." She wrapped her arms around herself as she shivered.

"Stay here with Kensy. I'll be back." I gently pushed her out of the booth so I could get out. I wanted to stay there and hold her, make sure she was okay, but I needed to find this asshole and deal with him first.

"You okay staying here with her?" Capshaw asked Kensy, already climbing out of the booth.

"Yeah, we'll be fine."

I helped Bella into the booth and waited until Kensy came around and sat next to her before I went with Capshaw in search of this guy.

"I'll head out front. You search in here," he said, immediately taking the same tone he used when we went on calls.

I nodded and started working my way through, looking for anyone who met Bella's description.

A few minutes later, I had cleared all of the tables inside, as well as the people in line to order. The bathroom was empty, and no one was lingering in the hallway. I pushed through the double doors and headed outside where I found Capshaw walking toward me. He shook his head and I felt the anger rise inside me that this guy didn't get the ass beating he deserved for freaking Bella out.

"We should get going," Capshaw said, not needing to say anything more.

"Agreed."

We both knew if we stuck around and spotted the guy, the chances were high that we would beat the living shit out of him. Not only that, but what was more troubling was that this guy was watching Bella, and I wasn't going to let it continue if I could help it. We could call the police, but not having a good enough description of him would be a waste of their time since he was already gone.

We went back inside, grabbed some to-go containers for the food, and headed back to my house.

Bella was still pretty shaken up by the time we got there, so I told Capshaw we were going to call it a night. Kensy said they understood and to let them know if we needed anything. It felt weird to be responsible for taking care of someone else, but I couldn't imagine *not* being there for Bella right now.

When I went inside, she was curled up on the couch with a blanket wrapped around her. I put our food in the fridge until she was ready for it and sat down beside her. I could tell she was still struggling with what happened, so I pulled her into me and held her as she cried.

"This is so stupid," she sobbed a little while later, lifting her arm to throw away her tissues in the trashcan beside us.

"It's not stupid," I assured her. "It's okay to be upset about what happened."

"Yeah, but nothing actually happened." She leaned forward and turned to face me. "He didn't attack me or anything, just creeped me out with what he said. But I should be used to it, it's not like he's the first guy to ever talk to me like that."

"That doesn't make it right. If anything, it just makes the list longer for me."

"List? List of what?" she asked, tilting her head to study me.

"People whose asses I'm going to kick."

Her head tipped back slightly as the most beautiful sound of laughter came floating out of her mouth.

"Thank you. I needed that."

"You're welcome, but I'm serious. I'm starting a list of asses to kick."

"You don't need to do that. It'll be never-ending and just comes with the territory of what I chose to do with my life."

I shook my head, trying not to let my anger get the best of me.

"No, Bella. Don't give anyone an excuse to treat you like that because of what you do. If they don't like it, that's their problem. But they don't get to run their mouth to you about it. That's where I come in."

"My knight in shining armor," she said softly with a smile.

"You bet your ass. I'll always protect you, Bella. No matter what. That's what you do for the people you love." The words were out of my mouth before I could think about it.

Her head whipped up as her eyes scanned my face, trying to read whether I was lying.

"I don't regret saying it," I assured her immediately. "And I would rather say it to you the first time while we're by ourselves than to do it in front of everyone as we get married. I love you, Bella."

Her face softened as tears filled her eyes. She smiled softly at me as if I just gave her the greatest gift ever.

"I love you too," she replied, leaning over to kiss me.

I reached over and grabbed her, pulling her back against my chest where she belonged. While I was already planning to tell her how much I loved her when I said my vows, I was happy to have been able to tell her in private first. That way, she didn't have to wonder whether it was sincere or just for show.

182

Twenty-Nine
Bella

It had been a few days since the encounter with the creep at Tipsy Taquito, but I couldn't shake the feeling that someone was watching me. I'd been paranoid all week but tried to hide it the best I could. For all I knew, everyone just assumed I was a nervous bride getting ready to take the plunge into holy matrimony.

"You look weird," Lia said, studying me over the top of her coffee cup before taking a sip.

"Gee, thanks."

"You know what I mean. You're beautiful—as always, but something is off. What's going on."

"Nothing," I lied, lifting my cup and taking a drink.

"Bullshit. I know you better than anyone. Are you having second thoughts about the wedding? Did Jones do something that I need to go break his femur?"

"No, he didn't do anything."

"So then you're having second thoughts about getting married," she said matter-of-factly.

I shook my head because even though I was more bothered by what happened the other night with the creep, I couldn't sit here and lie about not second-guessing this whole marriage thing.

"Everything is going to be fine, Bella. I promise. Jones is a really great guy. You guys seem so comfortable with each other already. The marriage part is just to make it official for the inheritance."

"I know." I sighed heavily, letting my shoulders fall. "But Lia, I'm taking something important away from him. What happens if we get divorced, and then he falls in love with someone else and wants to get married? I'll have already stolen all the firsts for him, so his real wedding won't be as special because he's already done it."

"Do I need to get a dirty sock?" she asked, raising her eyebrows.

"No, *Kensy*. Geez, what is it with you guys and dirty socks? Do you have some weird kink I never knew about?"

"I have plenty, but dirty socks are not one of them. And you're missing the whole point here."

"Okay, what's that?"

"You're so focused on convincing yourself that this is a fake marriage that you won't stop and allow yourself to consider that Jones might be considering this a *real* marriage. So, while you're obsessing over how he might feel in the future, you're not thinking about how he feels about it right now. Who knows, maybe this is how things are supposed to be, and you're only making it more complicated by fighting it."

I shook my head, not wanting the words to settle in my brain. If they did, they would plant seeds there, and then thoughts of having a future with him would run wild, and I wouldn't be able to rein them back in when he changed his mind about all of this.

"So, what's on the agenda for today?" I asked, changing the subject.

Even though I had lived here with Lia longer than I lived with Jones, it didn't feel like home anymore. I knew where everything was, but it didn't have that feeling deep down inside me that felt like I belonged there. Not like how I'd felt this week staying with Jones.

"Kensy will be here shortly, then we're running out to pick up the dresses and flowers. We'll drop some stuff off at the fire station, then we have some surprises lined up."

My brow immediately furrowed.

"What kind of surprises?"

"If I told you, they wouldn't be a surprise, now would they?" She gave me a look as she passed me to set her cup in the sink. "I'm going to jump in the shower. Feel free to make yourself at home."

I sighed dramatically, making sure she could hear it before she left, and then made my way to the couch after refilling my coffee cup. I didn't feel like watching TV, so I scrolled through social media on my phone until a new text message from Jones popped up.

Jones: How's your morning going, beautiful?

My cheeks burned with how tight the smile stretched across my face just seeing his name.

Me: Good. How's yours?

Jones: It would be better if you were here.

I was about to reply but stopped when his next text came through.

Jones: Never mind, I take that back.

Oh. Okay. Kinda harsh, but at least he's being honest.

I tried not to let the hurt wash over me, but it was there, in waves, as I tried to think of another way he could have meant that. Is he happy that I'm not there? Is his life better *without* me in it?

Jones: It would be better if you were here and my cock was buried deep inside you.

My fingers moved quickly over the screen, but a picture message popped up before I could get my reply out.

"Fuck," I muttered to myself, pulling at the light hoodie I was wearing as my body heated up.

I pinched my fingers on the screen and spread them, making the image of his hard cock larger so I could zoom in on the tip. Right there, where my mouth should be, was a drop of precum glistening like a beacon calling to me.

Me: That's not fair. You know how much I love him. He's ready and waiting for me to suck that precum off.

Jones: He's definitely ready. But we can't do anything until tomorrow night, after the wedding. Remember?

Me: I think the wedding day counts. I can come over at midnight, and we can seal the deal at 12:01.

Jones: Nope. You asked for this. I'm just showing you what you're missing out on until then.

Me: You're so mean.

Jones: Don't worry, all of this build-up will work in your favor tomorrow.

Me: Tomorrow is too far away.

Me: I guess you leave me no choice but to go to Jaxson. He knows what I like.

Jones: WHO THE FUCK IS JAXSON

Me: Oooh, jealous much?

Jones: No.

Jones: Possessive as fuck.

Jones: WHO IS JAXSON

Me: Don't worry, you've met him before.

Jones: I have a hard dick in my hand right now, Bella. Unless you want me to show everyone in town as I storm over there, I suggest you tell me.

Me: Oh my gosh, you wouldn't!

Jones: Try me.

Me: You're so grumpy when you're horny.

Jones: I'm waiting.

Me: You've already met him before.

Me: He's about ten inches long. Has a piercing…

Me: Knows how to get me off in seconds

Before I could press send, my phone started ringing. But it wasn't just Jones calling me; he was FaceTiming me.

"Hey," I answered casually as if I hadn't just told him I was planning to get myself off with his sworn enemy.

"Go to the bathroom," he instructed, the vein in his neck protruding.

"I don't really need t—" I started before he pinned me with a look and interrupted.

"Now."

"Yes, sir," I replied, a hint of mocking in my tone as I got up and headed toward the guest bathroom in the back of the house. "So bossy."

"You have no idea," he muttered, waiting for me to close and lock the door.

"Fine, I'm in the bathroom. Now what?" I held the phone in front of me, trying to ignore how hot he looked right now.

"You want something to get you off, fine. But I'll be damned if you use that fucking toy."

"What are you going to do about it? You already said sex is off-limits until tomorrow night after the wedding, and I hate to tell you, but I'm a very needy girl. And those needs are needing to be met before then unless you want a grumpy bride at the altar."

"First—I don't care how grumpy you are, Bella. I'll bend you over and fuck you for everyone to see. Try me. Second— your pleasure is mine, which means you don't get to get off unless I'm there to give it to you. Since you're already gone for the day and very *needy*, I'm willing to make an exception because that's the kind of *husband* I am."

"Alright, so what are you planning to do about this?" I sat down on the edge of the tub and stared at him.

"Take your pants off."

My brow quirked as I tried to process his words, but his strong hand gripping his cock and stroking it was a bit distracting.

"What?"

"Your pants, Bella—take them off. Hurry before you have to explain to Lia what you're doing."

"I'm not going to take my pants off."

He let his hand fall from his cock and sat up straight, bringing the phone closer to his face. His gorgeous, beautiful face with a strong jawline, dark green eyes, and plump lips that begged to be kissed.

"Bella," he said, clearing his throat. "Stop thinking about me eating you out and focus for a minute."

I shook my head, hating that he could read me so easily.

"I've made it very clear that the only person who gives you pleasure is me," he said sternly, his Adam's apple bobbing. "Your orgasms are mine, and you will come when I say you will. Do you understand?"

I nodded, my lower lip stuck in between my teeth.

"I'm saying you'll come now, so take off your pants."

My heart raced in my chest as I considered what he was saying. It wasn't like anyone was around to hear me, but I'd also never had phone sex with someone who could watch what I was doing.

"Now."

Breaking from my trance, I stood up and set the phone on the vanity as I pulled my leggings down my legs and tossed them to the floor.

"Panties?" I asked, speaking down to the phone, knowing he couldn't see me since it wasn't aimed at me.

"Leave them on."

"Okay," I said shakily, picking up the phone and feeling calm again as I looked at him.

"Are you wet for me, baby?"

I wanted to lie and say no, but there was no use. I could tell he already knew. I nodded and felt a chill creep over me as I imagined him there, pleasuring me.

"Take your shirt off," he instructed, lowering his phone so I could see him stroking his cock again.

I set my phone on my knee and pulled it off, tossing it to the floor.

"Tank top and bra as well."

I did as he asked, then lifted the phone, not sure how I felt seeing my bare breasts on the screen in the bottom corner where my face should have been.

"Fuck, Bella. I wish I were there to suck those nipples the way you like. I could make you come quicker than that damn toy. Rub them for me; show me how hard they get."

Holding the phone steady with one hand, I used the other to roll my nipple between my fingers, moaning softly at the ache starting to build.

"Do the other one."

I adjusted the phone so he could see as I worked the other one the way I liked.

"Do you see what you do to me, baby? Look how hard I am. I want to fuck you so hard, Bella, and then come all over your tits."

"I would love that."

"Show me your pussy. Let me see how wet she is for me."

I lowered the phone and spread my legs, letting him see the wet spot on my cotton panties.

"You're killing me, Bella."

"I could come over, and we could put each other out of our misery. Cancel the bachelor/bachelorette parties and just spend the day fucking," I offered.

"Nope," he said, voice strained. "We're sticking this out and waiting until tomorrow. You have no idea what's in store for you."

"Tell me," I whimpered, needing to hear his dirty words to spur me on.

"Slide your panties to the side first. Show me how wet your finger is when you slide it inside."

I tried to pay attention to where I aimed the phone as I gently pushed them aside and slipped my finger in.

"Ah," I cried out, already on the edge and desperate for relief.

I looked down at the screen to see him gripping his dick so hard it had to hurt.

"Add another finger in and fuck yourself with them."

I leaned back and did as he asked, nervous about the sound echoing through the small room as I plunged my fingers in and out as quickly as possible.

"Does that feel good, baby?"

"Mmmhmm."

"I'm close to coming, Bella. Come with me. Rub your clit and get yourself off."

I could hear the need in his voice and watched as he tried to control himself with slow, steady strokes.

"It's not going to take me long," I admitted, pulling my fingers out and spreading the wetness across my clit before I began rubbing.

"Come for me, baby. Just like you did when you sat on my face and let me eat your pussy. God, you tasted so good, and I can't get over the way you felt as you spasmed against my mouth."

My heart raced as my breathing increased, my body right on the edge as his dirty words did their job of sending me over.

"I'm going to come, Bella. But it's not going to be anything compared to what you get tomorrow after I make you my wife. I'm going to fuck you so hard and spread my seed all over you; you'll be dripping my cum for days."

"Shit," I hissed, my body tightening as my pussy spasmed against my fingers, riding out the orgasm. I tried to hold the phone as still as possible but couldn't focus on anything other than the beautiful sight of Jones coming, ropes of cum shooting up his stomach and onto his chest.

He brought the phone back up to his face and studied mine.

"Don't ever for a second think that just because we can't be together, I'm not going to take care of your needs, Bella. Now that that's taken care of get yourself cleaned up and enjoy your day. Lia and Kensy have some special things planned for you."

"Thank you, but I'm not going to be satisfied until I have *you* inside of me."

"Soon enough."

"Also, how do you know what's planned for me today?"

"I know everything except how to cook. But that's not the point. I do however know what they have planned for you today, and trust me, you're going to love it."

I eyed him suspiciously, wondering how he knew what the surprises were, then realized Kensy must have told Capshaw, who told him.

"What are you guys doing today?"

"I don't know. Capshaw won't tell me anything. Last I heard, there were rumors about hookers and drugs, but I don't know."

"What?" I asked, pulling the phone in closer as I glared at him. "There better not be any fucking hookers. I swear to God, Jones, if I find out you so much as *look* at another woman tonight, I will come over there and cut your dic—"

"If you do that, how will I ever fuck you with it?" He cocked his head to the side, giving me a look that could melt my insides.

I opened my mouth and then closed it in frustration when I didn't have an answer for him.

"Relax, baby, I'm just messing with you. But you're cute when you're jealous. You know that?"

"Shut up, I'm not jealous."

"Yes, you are, and I love it. Now go get dressed and enjoy your day. I'll talk to you later."

"Okay," I said, sighing with resignation. "You too."

We hung up, and I rushed to put myself back together so I didn't have to explain to Lia what I had been doing.

Thirty

Jones

"You have got to be kidding me," I groaned, tossing my head back and closing my eyes as we walked into the room. "*This* is what you planned for my bachelor party?"

Capshaw clapped me on the back and forced me inside as the guys scattered around me and grabbed a spot at one of the tables.

"A cooking class?" I asked, leveling him with a look.

"What? You're getting married and it's part of your husbandly duties to be able to provide for your wife. That includes cooking." Nate winked as he squeezed past me and grabbed an apron from the woman who looked more than thrilled to have a room full of firefighters for her class tonight.

"I don't think this is going to help." I let Capshaw lead me to a table in the corner with a counter behind us. I glanced over my shoulder and laughed. "Six fire extinguishers? Do you really think we need *six*?"

"I tried to tell him we didn't need that many," Rodriguez chimed in. "But then I remembered what happened with the burgers last week, and we all agreed it would be best to add a few more."

He nodded to the other side of the room, where another six were lined up.

I shook my head and tried to listen as the woman up front spoke to us like we were a bunch of kids. Which wasn't totally her fault, given that she primarily taught kids cooking glasses, and the guys had pulled some strings to get her to do a special one for us.

"Alright, tonight I'm going to teach you guys how to make something I like to call Marry Me Chicken. I thought it would be fitting as I heard someone is tying the knot tomorrow! Plus, this is the perfect dish for those *forgive-me* meals, as well. You know, just in case you need it." She winked but suddenly seemed to remember she was in a room filled with attractive men and blushed.

She went over the directions as Capshaw and I prepared and sauteed the chicken. I could tell which of the guys were already used to cooking at this level because they just breezed through it and tossed bottles behind their backs as if they belonged in an upscale kitchen in Las Vegas. Then there were the others who were still trying to figure out how to trim the chicken breast and were already ten steps behind. She walked around the room, checking on everyone as they worked.

"Do you really think this works?" Capshaw asked, slicing his breast down the middle and then separating them on the cutting board in front of him.

"Cooking?" I focused on mine, making sure not to cut my finger with the knife. "It seems to work for most people, not including myself."

"No, this whole *Marry Me Chicken.* Do you think if I make this for Kensy, she'll marry me?"

I stopped what I was doing and stared at him, royally confused.

"You guys are already engaged."

"I know, but she won't set a date, and I'm getting worried that she'll back out."

"Why? Has she said something?"

"No," he said with a heavy sigh as he washed his hands before getting the butter out and adding it to a large skillet. "But I don't know why it's taking so long. Look at you and Bella."

"Yeah, our circumstances are different." I lowered my voice, checking around to make sure no one was listening. "If we didn't *have to* get married, I don't think we would. Don't get me wrong, I really like Bella and have no problem marrying her. But I don't know that she would still want to get married if given the choice."

"I've seen you guys together. There's something real there. That chemistry is hard to find, and trust me, it's scary when you think of losing it."

"You're not going to lose it," I assured him. "I've also seen you and Kensy together, and I can tell you guys are meant to be together forever. She's going to marry you, she already said yes. I think it takes most people a while to plan a wedding. Maybe just give her some time for all of this to pass, then she can focus on planning her own."

"I don't know. I hope so. At least I'll have this Marry Me Chicken as a backup if needed."

I chuckled and patted his back as I thought about how nice it was to *not* be the one freaking out for once.

We took our time following the directions, and soon, the delicious aroma floating around us was proof that we were creating something incredible. Capshaw gave his undivided attention to the chicken while I took over making mashed potatoes. For the most part, that was uneventful if you ignored the fact that I started the hand mixer too high and shot butter and milk all over the cabinets above me. The woman leading the class gave me a wink and told me it happens all the time, but I wasn't sure that was much of a compliment, given that she worked with those who still struggled to tie their shoes.

I felt like I really shined when it came to steaming the asparagus. It probably wasn't rocket science to most people, but I was proud that they were soft yet firm, the perfect balance of lemon and salt bringing out their flavor.

While she mainly focused on kids' cooking classes, I was curious to see if she would also consider adding on a beginner-adult class. There were a million things I wanted to give Bella after taking her as my wife and being able to cook for her was one of them.

After the class was over and we all ate what we made, we headed to a local pub for some beer and hot wings for those who didn't have as much luck with their chicken. Thankfully, Capshaw and I had made ours to perfection, which was nice given there was more on the line for him than for me. I was just happy that we didn't have to use any of the fire extinguishers.

I sat and listened to the guys' bullshit as we drank a few beers, none of us interested in getting wasted tonight. I wasn't sure what Kensy and Lia had planned for Bella tonight, but I hoped it was as relaxing as my night.

Thirty-One

Bella

"I cannot believe you did this," I whispered loudly to Lia and Kensy as we sat at the back of the living room, watching the woman demonstrate how to give proper head to a cucumber. While the day had been nice with the spa treatment and full body massage, I had thought that was the end of the surprises. "Did Jones know about this too?" I asked, imagining what he must have been thinking when he found out.

"What?" Lia said, shrugging her shoulders. "You and Kensy are both getting married, and it's your wifely duty to know how to give good head. And no, no one knew but me. I planned this all by myself and kept it a secret. He only knew about the spa stuff."

"I give great head," Kensy said, holding her washed cucumber in her hand, gripping it as she frowned. "I don't even know where to begin with this thing. It's all crooked and lopsided."

"Well, they only had a small selection of decent cucumbers," Lia replied. "I bought what they had and then had to lie to the clerk about why I needed twenty of them. I'm pretty sure she knew what I was doing when she spotted the whipped cream and bottle of chocolate syrup in the cart too."

"You're not—" I started, already panicking.

"Oh, God, no. That's for ice cream sundaes after everyone leaves. Only the cucumbers are being violated tonight." Lia pretended to shudder as I noticed a dark blush creep across Kensy's cheeks as she quickly looked away.

I didn't want to be disruptive to the woman trying to show us the proper technique for taking a thin vegetable deep into our throat so I decided I would ask Kensy about that later. There was definitely a story to tell there.

"If you start gagging, you've gone too far," the woman said, though there was a mischievous smile tugging at her lips.

I turned my head and pretended to cough before getting up to grab my wine glass. I was pretty sure Jones wouldn't agree with that since we both knew that I gagged *right before* I got to the good part.

I couldn't figure out what Lia's true motivation was for organizing this oral sex workshop, but she'd gone all out by inviting a handful of friends and was now sitting up front so she could hear better. I sat down with Kensy, still sipping my wine as the other women took turns seeing how far they could take a cucumber.

"Do you think she did this for me or for herself?" I teased, nodding to Lia, who had her head back and was trying hard not to gag. The cucumber was barely in, but we giggled when we saw her throat moving, trying to force everything out. The teacher was patient and gentle with Lia, offering words of encouragement for her to keep trying.

"I think it's for her," Kensy replied, lifting her wine glass. "She needs to relax her jaw, or it's never going to go in right."

"She's already gagging, and it's barely in."

"Look, she's getting more in. Maybe she's got—"

We both stopped and watched as Lia pushed it in further with her finger, her face looking more relaxed than it had been before, then suddenly she pulled it out and started coughing.

"Never mind," we both said at the same time.

"Are you taking notes?" she asked, turning to face me as our cucumbers sat behind us. My stomach growled, and I considered eating it, but knew the teacher would be appalled if I did. She seemed fairly laid back and had a down-to-earth vibe, but I couldn't imagine she would approve of me eating them.

"About this?" I pointed to the crowd of girls still working on it. "Nah, I think I'm good."

"Same. And honestly, if Lia was trying to get something more realistic in size, she should have gone with eggplant."

I spun fully around to face her, my jaw dropping.

"Are you saying Capshaw is eggplant level?" I asked, lowering my voice the best I could.

She shrugged, but a sly grin spread across her cheeks.

"It would be pretty close."

"No shit." I nodded approvingly.

"What about Jones? Where does he lie in the produce department?"

"He's like one of those home-grown zucchinis. The ones that are long and thick, not the wimpy supermarket ones."

"Sounds delicious."

I giggled and covered my mouth as I looked at her.

"Sorry, I'm hungry, and the thought of eating fried zucchini got my appetite going."

"Same. I'm going to need real food soon. I'm tempted to eat this," I said, picking up the floppy cucumber and frowning. "Or maybe not."

I took another drink, enjoying the bitter taste of the wine on my tongue. The woman was still talking, somehow shifting into a conversation about women's pleasure as Lia hung on her every word. I picked up my phone and opened my text messages, finding the last one Jones had sent. I hadn't deleted the dick pic he sent earlier, but I also didn't want to get caught staring at it, so I typed out a new message and hit send.

Me: Your cock is better than all of the cucumbers in the world

I went to set it down on the counter behind me, assuming he was busy with the guys having his bachelor party, but it immediately dinged with a new message alert.

Jones: Should I be jealous of a cucumber?

My cheeks split as I grinned down at my phone.

Me: Not at all. You're so much better than a cucumber. You're a home-grown zucchini.

Jones: (scared eye emoji)

Jones: Do I want to know what you girls are doing?

Me: Probably not.

Jones: How are you?

Me: Missing you and your cock.

Jones: My cock and I miss you too.

Me: Are you enjoying your night? Are there any naked girls I need to worry about?

Jones: I am enjoying the night, and no, there are no naked girls. I have no desire to see anyone but you, Bella.

Me: (heart emoji)

I didn't think I'd had that much wine, but talking to Jones made me feel like I was drunk. He relaxed me in a way that I still didn't understand yet.

Me: I will let you go but just wanted to say I miss your zucchini. You really know how to use it.

Jones: I miss your pussy and can't wait to tend to your garden.

I laughed and put my phone away, trying to enjoy my last night as a single woman.

Thirty-Two

Jones

Today was the day. I was getting married and making Bella my wife.

I had been a nervous wreck since I got up this morning, thinking about all of the ways I could screw this up. But then I would think about Bella, and everything just felt right. It was unnerving how just the thought of her could calm me. How I had ever gotten lucky enough to get her attention, I would never know. But I was going to work hard every single day for the rest of my life to make sure I kept it.

The guys were already at the fire station when I got there, excitement buzzing around me as they worked to get it set up for us. Abby and her sister Jane had taken the lead, guiding everyone on where to put the chairs and how to arrange the flowers perfectly over the arch Rodriguez had built for us.

"This looks amazing," I said, stopping beside Abby and Nate and staring in disbelief.

It didn't even look like the same place I spent the majority of my time. Not only was it spotless and cleaner than I'd ever seen, but it was exactly what I had envisioned when

Bella told Kensy about what her dream wedding would look like the night we were there to plan everything.

Rows and rows of chairs were lined up with a light cream-colored runner for Bella to walk down the aisle. Pink and red rose petals had already been dropped along the side of the runner, leaving her path clear.

"Thank you," Abby said, inhaling deeply before looking at me. "We were hoping you guys would love it."

"Has Bella seen it yet?" I asked, already counting down the minutes until I could see her again.

"No, she wanted to be surprised. She's still at Lia's house getting ready. Kensy said they should be here in an hour."

"We've got the table over there set up for gifts and cards," Abby said, pulling my attention back to her when all I wanted to focus on was my bride-to-be. "And then we'll use that table for the cake. I finished it this morning but didn't want to bring it over until everything else was set up. I spoke with Capshaw, and he confirmed the food is already set for delivery from Surf 'N Shack to arrive after the ceremony, so I think everything is ready to go."

I nodded but couldn't get any words to come out of my mouth as my throat tightened and constricted around them. What if Bella changed her mind and decided not to go through with this? I would be left waiting for someone to love me—again, only for it to never come. I wanted nothing more than to be with Bella, but what if she realized she could do better than me? What if I wasn't enough for her?

I tried to take a deep breath to calm myself down, but as the thoughts raced through my head, so did my heart.

"Thanks for taking care of all of this, baby. It looks great," Nate said, hugging Abby and planting a kiss on her forehead. "I'm going to take Jones to my office until we're ready to start."

I looked up at him, a panicked look on my face, until I realized he wasn't about to reprimand me. He was saving me.

We stepped inside his office, where I began pacing wildly, my hands folded behind my head to keep from fidgeting as he shut the door and sat at his desk. He looked calm and relaxed while I resembled a wild animal, caged in and ready to flee.

I had been so excited this morning when I was just *thinking* about marrying Bella. But now that things were set up and a wedding was planned to happen in the next hour—I was losing my shit and second-guessing everything.

"What if I'm not what she wants?" I asked, looking for the answer I expected to see on his face.

The sympathy etched deeply into his smile as he shook his head no. Or the softness of his tone as he told me she changed her mind and didn't want me after all.

My stomach tightened, remembering all of the times I had gotten close to being adopted, but then it never happened. So many times I thought I would get my forever family, that I would have somewhere I belonged. But it always ended with me not being enough for them. I was a good kid, but they wanted someone else.

"You are what she wants," he said, kicking his feet up on his desk and resting his hands on his stomach.

He wasn't dressed yet—but neither was I—and that made me wonder if it was because he knew this wasn't going to happen after all.

"She could change her mind," I countered. "They always change their mind."

Nate shook his head, his energy still annoyingly calm.

"She's not going to."

"How do you know that?" I yelled in frustration, but he didn't even flinch. He was as cool as a cucumber. "Everyone always changes their minds when it comes to me, Nate. Why would she be any different?"

"I didn't change my mind." He shrugged.

"You and Abby are different." I closed my eyes and pinched the bridge of my nose between my fingers.

"I'm not talking about Abby," he said, putting his feet down and walking over to where I was standing. "I'm talking about you."

I furrowed my brow, no idea what he was talking about.

"When you first came on board as a rookie, they told me to trade you for someone else. To put you at another firehouse where you wouldn't make more work for me. To put you through hell until you gave up and quit."

"Why didn't you?" I asked, feeling even more defeated now.

"Because you belong here, Jones. You're part of our family. I knew it from the moment I saw you. You didn't get *stuck* here with us. You were *chosen*. I wanted you here. The guys wanted you here. Sure, it's taken a while for us to trust you around food, but we're getting there. My point is that there's nothing you could do that would make us feel any different."

I swallowed hard, trying to force the emotions down that were bubbling up inside.

"Well, thanks. But I don't think it works the same way for Bella."

He sat on the edge of his desk and folded his arms over his chest as he shook his head.

"Don't be so sure about that."

"What do you mean?"

"Bella is a lot like you. Whether she admits it or not, she's looking for where she belongs. For who will accept her for who she is. And Jones, you've shown up for her, time after time. You've already proven to her that you'll be there for her. You agreed to marry her without even thinking twice about it. There's no way that this isn't meant to be for you guys. I've seen you two together, and it reminds me a lot of Abby and me."

"I don't think I could handle if she changed her mi—"

"She won't," he interrupted. "Though, she might be disappointed if she shows up and her groom is wearing a t-shirt and joggers."

I looked down at what I was wearing, knowing she wouldn't be *totally* disappointed given how much she liked these pants.

"Let's get you married," Nate said, clapping my shoulder before grabbing the hangers from the hooks on the back of the door.

<u>Thirty-Three</u>
Bella

Don't trip and fall. Don't trip and fall. Don't trip and fall.

Music floated softly around me as everyone stood and watched me start down the aisle. Never had I felt so alone in my life than getting ready to take the plunge to get married and not have someone walk me down the aisle.

I shifted my bouquet in my hands and tried to swallow down the rising fear that was trying to wash over me. There was still time to turn around and run. I could skip town and avoid the embarrassment and drama of leaving an incredible man like Jones at the altar.

"Sorry I'm late," Capshaw said, rushing to stand beside me and offering his arm.

"What are you doing?" I whispered, looking up at him with tears in my eyes.

"You can't honestly think you were going to walk down the aisle by yourself," he said with a crooked grin.

"I didn't think about it until now," I admitted, pulling in a shaky breath.

I could feel everyone's eyes still on us and was thankful that it was a relatively small ceremony, with only close friends, as neither of us had family we wanted to attend.

"Are you ready?" he asked softly, giving me all the time in the world.

I wanted to scream *no* and reconsider why I was doing this, but then I saw Jones standing at the front next to the altar, and everything changed. My heart raced, and my feet started moving on their own accord.

I vaguely heard Capshaw chuckle as he led me down the aisle, but my attention was solely focused on the man I would soon call my husband.

Once we got to the front, we stopped, and the battalion chief asked something about who was giving me away today. Capshaw answered and then slid my arm out of his and placed my hands in Jones's.

I was still riding the insane emotional ride of being out of my mind freaked out about this and over the moon excited. I couldn't figure out which direction I was going, but when he smiled at me, I knew it wasn't anywhere without him.

Just as the battalion chief started talking, I had a moment of panic rush through me, my hands immediately dropping from his. His brow furrowed in concern as he studied me.

I'm about to marry someone who I don't even know their name. How do I introduce him to people? This is my husband, Jones—don't ask for his first name because I didn't bother to get it before I spread my legs for him. That's me—a girl who doesn't bother with the little details before jumping into bed with someone and agreeing to marry them! My grandma would be so disappointed!

"Are you okay?" he leaned in and whispered in my ear.

Thankfully, this wasn't a stuffy, formal reception where we had to be quiet and not speak to each other until we were officially married. My eyes snapped up at Jones, then looked over at the wonderful man trying to get us married.

"Take a minute if you need it," the battalion chief said, his voice filled with kindness that made me feel guilty I hadn't known his name.

I offered an awkward smile and then turned my attention back to Jones. Everyone was staring at us, the room so quiet you could hear a pin drop.

"What's the matter, baby?" Jones asked softly, pulling me closer to him so no one else could hear our conversation.

I leaned up on my tiptoes, trying not to topple over in my heels, and whispered in his ears.

"Um, I just realized that I am about to marry you and don't even know your name," I admitted, feeling my cheeks heat with embarrassment. As if that wasn't bad enough, I had worn my hair up, giving my face and neck a clear view for everyone to see the blush wash over me. I hadn't worn heavy makeup, wanting a more natural look, so I couldn't count on that helping either.

"Matt," he replied, his lips tickling the shell of my ear. "But you can call me whatever you want when I'm in between those legs as soon as he pronounces us husband and wife."

His finger trailed down my arm before reaching for my hand and holding it.

"Are we ready to proceed?" the battalion chief asked, looking between us.

I nodded and hoped he would ignore the scarlet flush on my cheeks as I reacted to Jones' dirty words.

The ceremony was quick, just like we had asked. I was all for doing the standard stuff and not writing our own vows, but Kensy and Lia had convinced me otherwise. It still felt weird since this wasn't a real wedding, but being able to convey my emotions to Jones made it feel worth it.

I stood there nervously, waiting as Jones cleared his throat before saying his vows to me.

"Bella, I've spent my life trying to figure out where I belong and longing to be loved. Then you walked in and changed everything I thought I ever wanted. You love me in a way no one else ever has. You're the calm to my storm. The light to my darkness. The reason I look forward to a new day every morning. I promise to love you unconditionally, to support you in every way I can, and to protect you from anything that wishes to do you harm. I will stand beside you today and every day for as long as we both shall live. And I promise you will never go a single day without feeling my love."

He pulled his lip between his teeth, and I knew what he really meant by that. Out of everything he said, that was the part of his vows that made me go weak in the knees. Our sex life was great already, but it had been a very *long* six days since I'd been with him, and I was ready to wrap this wedding up so he could make good on his promise to take me in my wedding dress.

He slipped the ring on my finger and squeezed my hand tightly.

"Jones," I said, my voice wavering as I started mine. "I never knew I could fall so quickly in love with someone, but with you, I never stood a chance. You've shown up for me in ways I never knew I needed. You've stood up for me countless times and have shown your unwavering support with things that others look down upon. I never feel like I have to prove anything to you, and you calm me in a way that no one else ever has. You're the person I turn to for comfort. The one I go to when I need to laugh. You give me things I never knew existed," I added, lowering my voice. I could see his eyes darken, knowing he was picking up on my hidden meaning like I had with his. "I promise that I will always stand by your side and that you will never have to question where my loyalty lies. I cannot wait to call you my husband and to be the best wife you could ever ask for."

I took the ring from Lia with shaky fingers and slipped it over his finger, making it official.

His grin spread across his face as he reached over and grabbed me by the waist, pulling me into his chest as he lowered his lips against mine.

"Umm, you may now kiss the bride," the battalion chief said as everyone started applauding and cheering for us.

My cheeks felt tight from how big my smile was stretched across my face. I wasn't sure I could do a fake marriage, but now that it had happened, I wasn't sure how I would ever be able to walk away once this was done.

Thirty-Four

Bella

"Okay, we've cut the cake and eaten some. Now I want to eat yours," Jones growled in my ear with his hand splayed possessively across my stomach.

I giggled and spun around, popping another bite of cake into his mouth.

"So needy and impatient," I teased, licking the frosting off my finger painstakingly slow, teasing him even though I needed a release just as bad. I was getting ready to do the next one, but then he snatched my hand and brought my fingers to his lips, sucking the rest of the frosting off instead. My eyes widened, knowing we had an audience, although neither of us seeming to care.

"I've shared you long enough," he complained. "Dinner, the first dance, toasts, now the cake. I can't wait any longer, baby."

"Okay, okay," I said with another giggle. "But how do you suppose we sneak out of here without anyone noticing?"

"That's easy." He reached down and grabbed me by the back of my thighs, tossing me over his shoulder and carrying me out of the room fireman style as everyone whistled and hollered.

"JONES!" I shrieked, smacking at his back. "This isn't discreet at all!"

"Bella, my dick doesn't care about discreet. Be glad I have any restraint left right now. I would have gladly fucked you over the cake as they tried to cut it. I'm a man on a mission with balls bluer than the ocean—nothing is going to stop me."

He led us through the fire station the same way he had the other day, and as promised, we ended up in the same room. He flipped on the light, locked the door, and then deposited me on the desk as he loosened his tie.

"Hike your dress up for me, baby."

I wiggled around as I gathered the fabric and bunched it up over my hips, spreading my legs to show him the white satin panties I was wearing. Within seconds, he was across the room and kneeling in between my thighs as he pressed soft kisses against my throbbing, wet pussy. I knew the fabric of my panties was already wet, but I didn't care. The hunger in his eyes was enough to make me grip the back of his head and press him harder where I needed him.

He pushed the fabric aside and took his time teasing me with his tongue. Long, slow strokes along my slit followed by rapid flicks against my clit. He inserted two fingers in between my folds, forcing me to gasp at the sudden intrusion. I hadn't realized just how needy I was until now. Even though I teased him about getting myself off this week, I hadn't other than the few times we did together, because I knew nothing would ever compare to him.

"I missed this pussy," he murmured, licking up my wetness as he finger fucked me.

"She missed you too."

"Fuck, Bella, I want to fuck you so bad."

"Do it. Please. Right now. Fuck me," I panted, tipping my head back as I imagined him sucking my nipples.

"I will, baby, but first, you're going to come on my tongue."

He began sucking my clit, making my pending orgasm build. I pulled down the top of my dress, making sure not to tear the lace. As if sensing what I needed, he reached up and caressed my breasts through the matching satin bra, the friction making my nipples instantly hard.

Suddenly, he pulled his mouth away from my pussy and stood up.

"You know I can't resist these beautiful tits," he growled, unhooking my bra with expert ease before dropping it to the floor. My breasts sat on full display, round and perky, as he licked his lips before drawing a nipple into his mouth. His finger rubbed my clit while he sucked, instantly bringing me to climax.

"Oh my God," I cried out, digging my nails into his arms as I tried to hold on while my body pulsated beneath him. "Fuck. Fuck. Fuck!"

"Trust me, baby, I'm going to fuck you in about two seconds."

Once I was done spasming against his fingers, he pulled them out and inserted them into his mouth, sucking my arousal off them. He extended his hand and helped me down before guiding me to turn around. I bent over the desk, hiking my dress up again as I heard him pull his zipper down. A few seconds later, the sound of the condom wrapper tearing filled the air as I waited impatiently for him to fuck me.

"I've waited too long for this," he said, lining himself up at my entrance as he pulled my panties to the side again. "Now I get to officially fuck *my wife*. I'm going to take it easy on you for now, baby, but once we're done here, I'm going to fuck you so hard."

He thrust inside, both of us moaning as my body immediately welcomed him back. His fingers gripped my hips tightly as he pulled out and slid in harder, pushing my hips against the desk as my breasts bounced freely.

"Give it to me hard now," I begged. "I can handle it. I want it."

"We don't have time for all of the stuff I want to do to you. So, for now, this is gonna have to do. Then we'll wrap up out there, and I can finally have you to myself."

I nodded my head, too caught up in pleasure to respond to him. He held on as he pinned me against the desk and thoroughly fucked me the way I loved.

<u>Thirty-Five</u>

Jones

We laughed. We danced. We drank champagne. But none of that mattered because all I wanted to do was get Bella into bed and claim her body over and over again as my wife.

I had told the guys they didn't need to do anything special for me, but they'd all pitched in to cover my shifts for an entire week so I could take Bella to a lake house in New Hampshire for a mini honeymoon until we could go on our real one to Italy in six months. It turned out that Rodriguez's family owned it, but it wasn't currently being used because his parents were traveling through Scotland. I didn't know that on top of booking us a honeymoon suite at the local hotel tonight, they'd also arranged for a limo to take us there, as well as pick us up to take us to the airport tomorrow morning.

If someone would have told me years ago that this would be my life right now, I wouldn't have believed them. There was no way a guy like me—someone who had always drawn the short end of the stick—would luck out with the most beautiful woman in the world as his wife and a brotherhood who selflessly gave whatever they had. It might have started as a fake marriage for Bella to claim her inheritance, but damn if it wasn't feeling more and more real by the minute.

Once we got to the room, I stopped and pushed our luggage to the side before swiping the card in the reader to open the door. A clicking noise sounded before the light turned green. I grinned at my beautiful bride, then lifted her into my arms as I carried her over the threshold. She giggled as I spun her around, joy overwhelming me that she was officially mine.

Before we got too dizzy, I set her down, making sure she was steady on her feet before going back to grab our luggage. Once I was back inside the suite, I put the Do Not Disturb sign on the door and locked every lock. Nothing—and I meant nothing—was going to keep me from my bride.

She wandered around the room, the bottom of her dress clutched in one hand to keep it from dragging while her heels dangled in the other. Her hair was down, cascading down her back in loose curls, stopping just above her ass.

I watched her as I undid the cuff links and set them on the nightstand, then loosened my tie.

"This room is beautiful," she said softly, running her fingers lightly over the fabric of the plush white comforter on the bed.

"Nothing is as beautiful as you."

She grinned her beautiful smile, her eyes lighting up the way I loved when she was truly happy.

I stalked over to her, grabbing her shoes and tossing them to the floor as I pulled her into me. My mouth crashed down over hers, desperate to taste her. She let go of her dress and wrapped her arms around my neck, deepening the kiss.

I lifted her to my hips, grinning when she eagerly wrapped her legs around my waist and locked them behind my back. I walked us the few steps to the bed and laid her down gently as I climbed on top of her and continued making out with my wife.

"I want to freshen up real quick," she said, pulling away slightly to get her words out while I trailed hungry kisses down her neck.

"Later," I murmured, more interested in the here and now.

"Jones," she said with a giggle, shoving at my chest. "I have another surprise, and I promise you'll like it."

"But I already love this," I objected, my hands desperately rubbing over her body.

"We have all night. Give me a few minutes, and I'll be right back."

I sighed dramatically and rolled over, letting her up. She crawled across the bed, grabbed the duffle bag from the corner where I'd set all the luggage, and pulled an envelope out.

"Here, these should hold you over until I come back." She winked and handed it to me.

My heart raced as I sat up, quickly opening it as she slipped inside the bathroom and closed the door. My throat became dry as I stared at the sexy photos Bella had taken in my gear. I had already seen the one she had given me a sneak peek of with the black bodysuit and the turnout pants, but the rest were even racier than I could have imagined.

I flipped through the prints eagerly waiting to see what the next revealed, stopping when I came across one of Bella wearing a red leather corset that pushed her breasts up. The photo was taken at an angle, and I was instantly jealous of whoever it was that was lucky enough to get this shot because Bella's legs were spread as she looked down at the camera, her waxed pussy on full display in the crotchless panties she was wearing. Thankfully, I knew it had been Kensy and she was probably used to this kind of thing, given she did boudoir photography regularly, but still, I was jealous nonetheless.

The blood rushed past my ears so hard, the whooshing sound almost masking the noise the door made as it opened when Bella stepped out of the bathroom. She was wearing the same lingerie I had just seen in the photo, with the same sexy stilettos. She leaned against the doorframe, making no effort to come over to me as if my dick wasn't about to explode any second.

"Did you like the photos?" she asked casually, nodding to the stack that had fallen into my lap. "I was going to give them to you last night as a pre-wedding gift, but the girls and I got a little distracted."

"It's a good thing you didn't give them to me last night," I replied, my voice gruff.

"Why's that?"

"Because we would have missed the wedding today as I continued to fuck you senseless all night and through the day." I tossed the photos to the side and got up, crossing the short distance to get to her.

"This fucking outfit, Bella," I growled, my hands running over the leather.

"You don't like it?" she asked, pouting her full lip that I wanted to bite.

"I love it, but I would love it even better if my cock were sliding inside that sweet pussy of yours."

"Well, then, what are you waiting for?" She batted her eyes playfully before wrapping her arms around my neck and bringing her mouth to mine.

I lifted her to my hips and carried her to the bed, groaning against her lips as I felt the warmth between her legs against my body. I gently lowered her to the bed, stripped off my clothes, then climbed up to join her.

"I don't know how long I can wait to be inside you," I admitted, sitting up against the headboard.

"I'm wet and ready for you. We don't need to wait any longer." She climbed over my lap, positioning herself so her back was against my chest as she gripped my erection and stroked. I gripped her hips and guided her as she lowered herself over my cock.

"Fuuuccckkkk," I hissed out, holding her steady for a second.

She glanced back at me, dark eyelashes fluttering as her hair fell over her shoulder.

"What's wrong?"

"Nothing," I breathed out, pinching my eyes shut. "I've never fucked without a condom before."

"Oh! Sorry! Want me to grab one?"

She started to climb off until I dug my fingers deeper into her hips to keep her there.

"No, I wasn't lying when I said you would be dripping my cum down your legs for days, Bella. I don't want us to use condoms if you're comfortable with it. I get tested regularly when I go for my annual physical. I'm clean."

"Me too," she said quickly. "And I'm on birth control."

"For now," I muttered under my breath, already feeling the possessive urge to plant my seed deep inside her. "I just need a moment to get used to how fucking good you feel without wearing a condom. I don't want to blow my load within seconds."

She nodded as if she completely understood, then leaned back against my chest while I was still buried deep inside her. She pulled her hair over her shoulder and nestled her head beneath mine as she took my hands and guided them over her breasts. The leather was soft beneath my skin, but I could still feel her pebbled nipples through it.

"Your body is amazing, baby," I whispered in her ear. "You feel so good."

"You too. I love your big cock and how it fills me."

I lifted my hips, thrusting deeper inside her.

"This cock is yours, baby. I'm going to make you feel good every day and every night, starting now."

She whimpered and spread her legs further, allowing me to slide in further. I pushed forward so my chest was still against her back and waited for her to brace herself on the bed with one hand while I gripped her thigh to hold her where I wanted. I thrust up and moved slowly, enjoying the way her body felt as I did more than just fuck Bella. For the first time, I made *love* to my *wife*.

230

Thirty-Six

Bella

I rolled over and stretched, forgetting Jones was beside me, as I accidentally smacked him in the face.

"Ow."

"Oh my God! I'm so sorry," I flipped over and covered my mouth, feeling terrible about the loud thud, knowing I walloped him.

"It's okay, I'll get used to it," he grumbled sleepily, grabbing me by the waist and pulling me into his chest.

"I haven't been in that deep of a sleep in a long time. I completely forgot where I was, and obviously that I wasn't alone. I can make it up to you." I wiggled my eyebrows seductively as he opened one eye and peeked at me. Just then, his phone started ringing on the nightstand beside him.

He reached over to grab it, fumbling around because he refused to let go of me.

"Yeah," he answered, the sleep still heavy in his voice. "What? Oh shit. That sucks. I'm sorry, man."

I felt my brow pinching, wondering what was happening on the other line.

"Nah, don't worry about it. We're good, but thanks."

He hung up the phone and set it back on the nightstand.

"Everything okay?" I asked, trying not to be too nosey.

"That was Rodriguez. Unfortunately, the lake house is flooded, and the neighbors are trying to deal with the broken pipe. We're not going to be able to go up there after all. I'm sorry, baby."

"It's okay. I still have the rest of the week off, so I'll spend it however I can, as long as I'm with you."

"Well, I'm still technically off too. I can see if we can stay here another night if you'd like?"

"Sounds good to me. We should call and cancel the flights before it's too late."

"No need to. Rodriguez already took care of it. I'm guessing he either knew someone there who handled it for him, or he just pretended to be me. I swear, that guy and his family have connections for everything."

"Well, think about what you'd like to do today. I need to pee, and then I'm going in search of food. You wore me out last night and left me famished this morning," I teased, pushing the blanket off me so I could get up.

"How about you go pee, and I'll order room service."

"We can't just stay cooped up in this room all day." I laughed, though looking at his toned naked body in bed, I wouldn't mind if we did.

"Want to bet? I have plenty of ways to keep us entertained."

"Do they all involve your cock?" I stood at the door to the bathroom and looked at him over my shoulder.

"No."

I frowned before I could stop myself.

"Some include my fingers and mouth."

The look he pinned me with had my insides flipping as heat jolted through my body.

****

After breakfast, we had sex, followed by more sex and a shower. My body was sore, and even though I hadn't had my fill of Jones yet, I had to give it a break. We sat in bed watching movies while I checked my emails on my phone.

Even though I was supposed to be off this week, it was just habit for me to check them every Sunday so I knew what was happening that week. There was a congratulatory email from Burt with a picture he had taken of the front page of the Beaumont Creek Gazette.

I smiled as I replied, assuring him that I would get the marriage certificate filed tomorrow. At least that would be off my plate and one less thing to worry about.

I was about to close my email when a new one popped up in my inbox. I didn't recognize the sender, but clicked it open after reading the subject line.

From: SPB0785964@email.com

Subject: Big Mistake

Date: May 20, 2024 1:57

To: bsanchez87@email.com

You shouldn't have done that. You really shouldn't have done that.

I swallowed hard, trying to push the discomfort aside as a chill ran through me.

"What's wrong?" Jones asked, immediately picking up on it.

I turned my phone to show him the email, watching as his eyes narrowed and his brow furrowed.

"Who sent that to you?"

"I don't know." My eyes widened as I shook my head. "I've never gotten an email like that before."

"Maybe it's a spam email?" he offered, though we both knew it wasn't.

"But there wasn't a link to click or anything like that. It feels personal."

A few seconds later, my phone dinged, alerting me to a new email. We both looked down and my body stiffened when I noticed it was from the same email address.

From: SPB0785964@email.com

Subject: And the bride wore white...

Date: May 20, 2024 1:58

To: bsanchez87@email.com

Did your husband *know you weren't a virgin before he married you? Or did you lie to him like you do everyone else? Sooner or later, your lies will catch up to you, and everyone will know you didn't deserve to wear white at your wedding. Everyone will know the truth.*

"What the fuck?" Jones growled beside me, wrapping an arm protectively around me. "Can you block them so they can't email you anymore?"

"Yeah, this isn't the first person I've had to do that with." My fingers moved quickly across the screen, immediately blocking the email address.

"Have you gotten messages like that before?"

"No, never like that. Usually, they're either hitting on me and trying to get me into bed, or they're from women who want to make sure I feel ashamed for what I do."

"I hate this for you," he replied, shaking his head. "I don't hate what you do. I hate that people feel like they have a right to talk to you this way."

"Me too," I admitted, setting my phone down beside me.

Usually, I would try to ignore the hateful messages and move on with my day, but this one felt worse. It felt more personal, and whoever had sent it knew about the wedding yesterday. Which wasn't a big deal because the entire town was talking about it, and the pictures had made the front page of the newspaper. But this felt different—more menacing, and that was a feeling I couldn't shake.

Thirty-Seven

Jones

I didn't sleep well last night, and it wasn't because I was worn out from pleasuring my wife all night. No, it was because I couldn't get over the disgusting emails she had received. I wished that the coward didn't hide behind some coded username so I could find who it was and go kick their ass.

Monday morning, we checked out of the hotel and returned our luggage to the house before I went with Bella to run errands. We needed to get the marriage certificate dropped off so they could file it, and then I promised her we would go grocery shopping and spend the rest of the day at home. I could tell she was still bothered by the email, and so was I.

While I didn't want to push Bella to be out if she didn't want to be, I also didn't want to encourage her to hide just because some creep online was being a douchebag. I was there to protect her and wasn't planning to leave her side any time soon.

"Do you want to grab lunch before heading to the store?" I offered, holding her hand as we walked to my truck.

"Sure." She smiled, but I noticed how it didn't meet her eyes as she glanced around the parking lot, making sure there wasn't anyone to worry about.

I held her tighter and guided her to the truck, helping her in before closing the door and going around.

It was quiet at Rockin' Rooster when we got there, with most of the crowd having already come through this morning for breakfast pastries and coffee. We placed our orders, and then I sent Bella to grab a table while I waited for our food.

I was talking to the lady at the register, just making small talk while our food was being finished when I heard the panic in Bella's voice as she called my name. I rushed over to find her at a table by the window, hand trembling as she pointed out the window.

"What's wrong?" I asked, bending down to see what she was staring at.

"That's the guy from the other night," she said, pointing to a guy walking away with a hoodie pulled over his head.

"Are you sure?"

She nodded, her face white as a sheet.

"Stay here," I commanded before darting out the door and running down the crowded sidewalk to catch up with him.

Just like the other night, he vanished into the crowd without leaving a single trace behind.

****

By the time we got home, I could tell Bella needed a break. She had been rattled ever since she saw the creep, and I hated that I hadn't been able to find him. In a sea of people, it should have been easy to find someone wearing a hoodie, given how warm it was outside, but by the time I rounded the corner on Main Street, he was gone.

I didn't want to take the time going into every store looking for him when I knew that Bella was upset. While I wanted to find the guy and figure out what his problem was, I wasn't willing to leave my wife in the state she was in. It was my job to take care of her, and that meant being there for her however she needed me.

"Hey, baby, how about a warm bath and a glass of wine?" I offered, rubbing her shoulders as she stood in the kitchen staring blankly out the window.

"I can make dinner," she offered, but I could feel the weight of the world sitting on her shoulders.

"How about I deal with dinner when you're done soaking? I'll bring you some snacks so you don't get too hungry."

She turned and wrapped her arms around my neck, smiling at me.

"I'm going to gain so much weight being married to you," she teased.

"Nah, I know plenty of ways for us to work it off."

I smacked her ass and grabbed the stuff I had picked up at the store before heading to the master bathroom. I wasn't sure how hot she wanted the water or when she would be ready to get in, so I went with a few degrees hotter than I liked and filled the tub with the rose-scented Epsom salts she had been looking at before pouring in the matching bubble bath.

A few minutes later, she came in carrying a glass of her favorite wine and set it on the counter. She stripped her clothes off, but it was solely so she could get in the bath, not to seduce me—which I didn't need right now. I wanted her to feel better however I could make that happen.

Once she was naked, she grabbed her wine and stepped into the water. I opened my mouth to warn her that it was hot, but she sank down without a care in the world and let the bubbles wash over her. Her eyes closed, and I watched all of the tension start to disappear.

I closed the door and gave her privacy while I got to work in the kitchen, praying I could recreate the Marry Me Chicken without setting the house on fire.

Thirty-Eight

Bella

"You know, you don't have to make me Marry Me Chicken since we're already married," I teased, taking another bite. I giggled the night of our bachelor/bachelorette parties when he told me they had taken him to a cooking glass, but there was nothing funny about the delicious meal he had made for me tonight. It was so good that I even looked around to see if there were any take-out bags, wondering if he had it delivered while I was soaking.

"We can call it something else," he said shyly, lifting his fork to his mouth.

"Right now, I feel like we should call it Blow Job Chicken because that's what you're going to get after I finish devouring this. It is freakin delicious, Jones."

"Thank you. It feels weird being able to say I can cook something."

"You did good with the mishap a while back at work, too," I reminded him. "Seems maybe you're finally coming into your skills as a chef."

His cheeks blushed an adorable shade of red as he shoved a hand through his short hair. I knew he wasn't used to compliments so I didn't want to keep pushing him and make him uncomfortable. I truly enjoyed dinner and wanted to make sure he knew.

We switched topics and filled the silence, discussing what we needed to do before the official honeymoon to Italy in November. I wasn't sure what to expect, but it was exciting that he was going with me. I mean, it would be weird to go and not take him since he was my husband, but I also didn't want to just assume that he would be able to take that much time off from work.

After dinner, we cleaned up and cuddled on the couch. It was nice not having to worry about anything right now. We could just be us and enjoy our time still getting to know each other.

We were watching an action-packed movie when my phone dinged with a message. I grabbed it, thinking it would be Lia checking in since I hadn't heard much from her since Saturday. She was back to working eighty-plus hours a week and had been lucky to get off for the wedding. Instead, it was another email that made my stomach turn.

From: TSAN187@email.com

Subject: Did you think you could run?

Date: May 21, 2024 8:58

To: bsanchez87@email.com

Bella, Bella, Bella. Did you really think you could get rid of me that easy? You should know by now that I know everything about you—including where you're at. What you're wearing. What movie you're watching. Maybe your husband *can learn a thing or two about how to catch the bad guys with that mindless crap on TV. Tell him to at least try harder. You wouldn't want people to think your marriage was* fake*, would you?*

I tossed my phone down and buried my head in my hands as I cried. I felt Jones pick it up, and then the couch shifted as he jumped up and checked the windows and doors. He called someone, anger rich in his voice, but I tuned it all out as I struggled with why this was happening in the first place.

Thirty-Nine

Jones

"What the actual fuck am I supposed to do?" I demanded, slamming my fist on the kitchen table as Nate and Capshaw gave me space.

Bella was in the bedroom with Kensy, the one place I knew she would be safe. The curtains were always closed in there, and the only way in or out of that room was through the living room, where we would all see her.

"We've already reported it to the police," Nate said with a frustrated sigh. "But there's nothing they can do until he physically becomes a threat."

"I'm not going to let that fucking happen."

"I know. We're not either," Capshaw assured. "We're going to do whatever it takes to catch this asshole."

Nate flipped through the emails I had Bella print out earlier, including the ones from the address she had blocked yesterday. We had her iPad sitting on the table, logged into her email, waiting to see if anything else came in.

"Whoever it is, they're determined. I don't think they're going to stop until they get whatever they want." Nate shook his head and pushed away from the table.

"But what is that?" I growled, my frustration mounting. "I swear to God if they do anything to hurt her—"

"They won't. We won't let them." Capshaw grabbed the papers, looking over them again.

We had all been through them at least a dozen times already, hoping that something would finally stand out and give us a clue as to who this was.

"I'm home this week, so I can watch her like a hawk, not let her out of my sight." I nodded, feeling like this gave me the control I needed.

"I was thinking," Capshaw said slowly, eyeing me cautiously before he spoke. "I think you should come back to work tomorrow.

"No. No fucking way." I shook my head vehemently.

"Hear me out—they're going to do whatever they're going to do—there's no stopping someone who is this determined. But the sooner things return to normal, the sooner it will happen. They're not going to be stupid enough to make a move while you're here with her."

"No!" I locked eyes with him, challenging him to change his mind.

"It's not a bad idea," Nate agreed, raising his eyebrows when I pinned him with an ice-cold glare. "Look, I know it's not what you want to hear. Trust me, I would lose my shit if something like this happened to Abby. But Capshaw is right. He's not going to make a move until he thinks you're out of the way. He already knows her routine—he's made that much clear. The sooner things go back to how they should be, the sooner he'll fuck up and do something."

"I've missed him *twice* while I've been out in public with Bella," I objected. "You're telling me you think she will be *safer* with me not around to help her? That's the stupidest fucking thing I've ever heard."

"*Neither* of us could find the guy that night, Jones. He's that good at hiding. I think the only way we're going to get ahead of this is to make him think he's in control when he's not."

"Who's to say it's even the same guy? It's a different email address, and you said Bella mentioned that she gets creepy comments from guys often. We could be dealing with two different guys."

"Exactly. And this one knew what she was doing. He's fucking watching her somehow in a place where she should feel safe. If I go back to work and leave Bella here by herself, how am I going to protect her?"

"You're not," Lia said, coming through the front door. "By the way, your window is open so the whole fucking neighborhood can hear you. Good job, GI Joe."

"What are you doing here? Aren't you supposed to be at work?" Capshaw said, folding his arms and studying his little sister.

"Yes, but Doctor Dickface let me leave early since there was a family emergency." She rolled her eyes.

"It's not an emergency," Capshaw objected, but she lifted her hand to stop him.

"I know you guys are married now, but you live further from the city than I do and don't have neighbors close by. She's safer living with me for a while until this is handled.

We have thin walls and nosey neighbors. If anything happens, they'll call it in." Lia sighed heavily, her eyes pleading with me.

<u>Forty</u>

Bella

"It feels weird to be here," I admitted, dropping my duffle bag on the floor in what used to be/was still my bedroom. "These past two weeks have been insane, and I feel like I don't even know which way is up at this point."

"You're telling me. I don't even know what our house looks like anymore. I've already gotten used to living at the hospital," Lia said, plopping down on the bed.

"When do you go back?"

"Tomorrow morning. I have to be there before seven to catch up on the stuff I missed leaving early today. Mostly just some paperwork, but nothing urgent. Doctor Dickhead was surprisingly kind about taking care of that for me instead."

"Maybe he likes you?"

"Please." She rolled her eyes dramatically. "That man doesn't like anything. He's the grumpiest person I've ever met."

"Besides you?" I teased, giggling as I ducked to avoid the pillow she tossed at my head.

"Hey, I have a good excuse for it. I'm sleep-deprived and haven't gotten laid in—I don't even know how long now.

It's like a drought down there, Bella. We need to call in federal aid to send some relief before there's a brush fire."

"I don't think that's how it works." I scrunched my nose. "But I could see if maybe Jones can get one of the other guys to spray you down with the hose."

She pretended to consider it, then shook her head.

"How are things going with you guys? I haven't had a chance to talk to you since before the bachelorette party. Even then, it's been so rushed with just a few words in between breaks."

I sighed heavily, sitting down beside her.

"It's going good. Really, really good."

I toed the rug beneath me to keep from looking at her until she nudged me with her shoulder.

"Awww! Does this mean you're finally having feelings for your husband?"

I rolled my eyes, but not nearly as dramatic as she did.

"Yes, I have feelings for my husband," I said sarcastically. "We actually said we loved each other before the wedding."

"You did?" Her teasing tone had changed to serious, and I was almost sure I could also hear a hint of hurt.

I nodded and looked at her.

"Why didn't you tell me?"

"I don't know." I shrugged. "Things started happening so fast after that. It was the night we went to dinner with Kensy and Capshaw, and I ran into that creepy guy in the hallway. We got home and I was crying and upset about it. He held me and threatened to make a list of people whose asses he needed to kick, then admitted that he loved me."

"I don't know if I'm more hurt that you didn't tell me right away when it happened or happy that my best friend is in love with her husband," Lia squealed.

"You know, a lot of people fall in love with their husbands. It's not 100% yet, but a recent poll showed that most newlyweds confirmed they loved their spouses," I teased, ducking when she grabbed another pillow and launched it at my head.

"Smart ass," she mumbled though it didn't keep the grin from tugging the corners of her lips.

"Better than a dumb ass." I winked, knowing she knew it was coming, as that was what we always said to each other.

"I know you probably miss your husband and all of the hot sex you guys were having, but I'm really happy to have you back for however long you need. I know I won't be here much, but at least the Hucklebees are home during the day and stay up late at night, so they'll hear if you need anything. And we all know how nosey Janet is. You can bet she'll call the cops if she sees anything suspicious."

I nodded and tried to smile, but what for? There was nothing to be happy about right now. Someone was blatantly stalking me, hiding in the shadows while I was left to sit and wait for them to make their move. On top of that, I had to be apart from the one person I wanted to be with the most right now.

252

Forty-One

Jones

While I would have loved to spend today at home with Bella, I was up early and reported to the fire station. Instead of working a forty-eight-hour shift like I usually did, I was only on for twenty-four hours so I could stay on track with my platoon. Yesterday was the start of their forty-eight on, but I was off for my honeymoon, which was now cut short. We didn't want to mess things up by having me work different days and with another platoon when we were trying to keep things as close to normal as possible.

But I also wasn't sure what I was supposed to do during my off time if Bella was staying with Lia and I didn't have to work for the next three days. How was that supposed to work if we were married but my wife wasn't living with me? People in town would start talking, and the last thing I wanted was to jeopardize her getting the inheritance because people questioned the validity of our marriage. Sure, it might have started out fake, but it felt more real than anything I'd ever felt before.

The guys were in the kitchen, eating breakfast, but my stomach had been sour since last night so I skipped it and went to check the supplies in the truck. I knew someone else had already done it, but I needed a task to keep my mind occupied so I didn't obsess over Bella all day.

As if knowing I was already thinking of her, my phone dinged with a text message alert.

Bella: I would say good morning, but it's only good when I wake up beside you. How are you?

Me: I barely slept last night and haven't been able to eat anything. Being away from you literally makes me sick.

Bella: I'm sorry. I haven't been able to eat either.

Me: I'm sorry, too. I wish there were more I could do. I hate being apart.

Bella: I'm the reason we're in this situation. I'm considering pulling out of my contract with Dark Vibes.

Me: Why would you do that? I thought you loved that job?

Bella: I do, but it doesn't make sense to keep doing it if it's going to put me and those I love in danger.

Me: We'll figure out who's behind those emails and stop it. Don't do anything you're going to regret, Bella. Just give me a little time to take care of this.

Bella: But we don't even know who it might be. It could literally be anyone—and even worse, we don't know if it's one guy or two. Hell, there could be several at this point. I haven't bothered to check my email since last night. My agent knows to call if she needs anything, but who knows what's waiting for me in my inbox?

Me: We'll take care of it.

Bella: But how? My getting married apparently triggered anger in some people around town. Who's to say when it will stop? Or if it will ever stop.

I was about to respond when Capshaw came in and nodded for me to head inside.

Me: I have to go; Nate is calling a meeting. I'll text you as soon as I can, but please don't do anything until then. Love you.

Bella: Love you too.

Forty-Two

Bella

I was going stir-crazy sitting at home, so I put on a movie and forced myself to try to watch it. But every time it got to a sappy love scene, I had to look away because it made the hurt in my heart that much stronger with how much I missed Jones.

It felt silly to be so upset about it, but at the same time, it felt like more than just missing him while he was at work. It was like something bigger had changed between us, and the promise of spending forever with him felt like it was now in jeopardy. It was a nagging feeling I'd had since the moment I woke up and was strong enough to make me throw up the food Lia tried to force me to eat.

Giving in to temptation, I went into my room to get my iPad out of my duffle bag, frustrated when it wasn't there. I must have forgotten it in the rush to get everything packed last night.

There was no way I was going to be able to sit around at home all day and not stress over what was happening, so I slipped on my shoes, grabbed my keys, and headed over to Jones's place to grab it. The least I could do while cooped up at Lia's house was figure out who was sending the emails. It was a short drive, and I would be back before anyone knew I was gone.

Forty-Three

Jones

Nate was talking about the situation and making sure the guys knew what was going on until we could get a handle on it, but I couldn't focus for shit with my mind constantly wandering to Bella. Just as he was about to wrap things up, the siren started, and we got the call to respond to a residential fire.

The second Lia's address came over the radio my heart leaped out of my chest as I rushed to get my gear on and get in the truck. It felt like it took forever to get there with more traffic on the streets than usual. Rodriguez leaned on the horn, forcing people out of our way, but every second that passed was one second too long before I could get to Bella.

I tried calling her repeatedly, but it kept going to voicemail, which made the knot in my stomach tighten even more when I thought about her being hurt—or worse.

By the time we pulled up outside the duplex, I had already climbed out and ran toward the house. I didn't need instructions on what to do—and honestly—I wasn't going to listen to any protocol right now. The woman I loved was in there, and nothing would stop me from getting to her.

I heard heavy footsteps beside me and didn't have to look to know that Nate and Capshaw were by my side. There was noise around me as the guys yelled commands, but everything went dead silent once the front door was forced open and flames rolled out.

I lifted my arm to block the heat, giving myself an eighth of a second to panic before rushing in and not looking back. Bella's life depended on me getting in there and getting to her before the fire did. I didn't have time to stop and think things through. The clock was ticking as her life hung on the line.

The thick smoke made it hard to see as I ducked low, feeling my way along the walls. Thankfully, I knew the house pretty well, which helped me navigate it quickly. I called out for her, knowing she probably couldn't hear me because she likely wasn't conscious unless she'd been able to get into another room and close the door before the fire spread.

I felt along the hallway walls, frustrated when all the doors were open. Finally, I reached where her room should be and felt for the doorknob. My heart raced when I realized it was closed, praying she was inside, waiting for me to come rescue her.

"Bella," I called out, trying to make myself loud enough for her to hear. "Bella, I'm here. Stay where you are. Don't open any doors or windows."

I waited for her to answer me, but before she could, I felt something heavy fall and hit my head as the roof began to collapse above me.

Forty-Four

Bella

The drive to Jones's house was quick, just like I expected. I got out of the car and walked up to the front door, the skin on my neck prickling the closer I got to the door. I tried to ignore it and reminded myself that everything was fine; I was just on edge from the past few days.

I took a deep breath, trying to hold the key steady in between my fingers as I reached for the knob. But before I could unlock it, the door slowly opened as it felt like the blood drained from my body.

"Todd," I gasped, clutching my hand to my chest and dropping my keys in the process. "What are you doing here?"

I took a cautious step back, patting my pocket to find my phone, but it wasn't there. My heart raced in my chest as I tried to figure out how to get away as he moved closer, pure evil in his dark eyes as he stepped outside.

"You and I both know the answer to that. You have something I want, and I've come to collect it."

I swallowed hard, wanting to run but knowing it wouldn't matter if I did. He was stronger. Faster. The closest neighbor wouldn't hear if I screamed for help. I was all by myself, at the mercy of my cousin, who wanted nothing more than to see me vanish so he could have his shot at my inheritance.

"You should really be more careful, you know," he said carelessly as if he had all the time in the world to be here. "Having your wedding photos posted all over town made it easy for me to get people to tell me where to find you. Many were surprised that you had a cousin you never talked about, but I was able to charm them all the same. They were so quick to give up the information I needed, and one older lady practically drew me a map of how to get here."

"Yeah, well, I don't talk about you for a reason. Why waste my precious energy telling people about what a manipulative asshole you are?" I knew I was just angering the beast, but honestly, what did I have to lose at this point? It wasn't like he was going to change his mind if I tried to kill him with kindness. I was biding my time, keeping him talking while I tried to figure out an escape plan.

"Whatever. Why don't we make this quick so I can get what I came for and get out of here."

"And what's that?" I continued to play dumb as I struggled to recall some of the basic self-defense moves I learned in that class Lia and I took a while back.

"You know exactly what I want, Bella," he hissed, clenching his fists at his sides. "None of that belongs to you. It's mine, always has been. Just because you sucked up to grandma in her last years doesn't mean you're entitled to any of it."

"I don't even want any of it," I replied with a snort. "I've never wanted anything from grandma and grandpa other than their time and company. I didn't ask her to leave me anything; she wanted to. And from the looks of it, she made the right decision."

His eyes narrowed even further as he worked his jaw back and forth.

"You better stop fucking playing with me, Bella. I'm not in the mood for it. Now we can do this the hard way or the—"

"There are no options for you, Todd," I growled, my built-up anger rising to the surface. "Everything is mine, and there's no way in hell you're getting any of it. I already got married before my twenty-fifth birthday. Now all I have to do is wait the six months and then collect everything."

"Not if you're dead."

His voice was so icy it sent a chill straight through me.

"Don't you get it, Bella? I'm not here to make small talk and catch up. I have one reason for being in this stupid small town. One problem to deal with. You. Now, why don't we take a quick walk in the woods over there so we can get this over with." He cocked his head to the side as he pulled out a gun and pointed it at my head as that nagging feeling from this morning settled in my stomach again.

Forty-Five
Bella

"Like I said, we can do this the hard way or the easy way," Todd said, moving closer as the gun brushed against my temple as I stood frozen in place. "You can be quiet and go easily into the woods back there so I don't have a mess to clean up, or you can be difficult and fight me on it. But we both know you're not going to win."

"No, mother fucker, *you're* not going to win," a deep male voice boomed from behind him, startling both of us.

Todd spun around, moving the gun with him just in time for me to see him point it at Nate.

"No!" I screamed as my instincts took over. Before I knew it, I was lunging in the air, my sole purpose to get the gun out of Todd's hand. I jumped on his back like a monkey, latched on the best I could, and pushed his arm so the gun was no longer aimed at Nate.

He spun around, immediately trying to get me off him, but I clawed and scratched until I could gain purchase and hold on. I reached for the arm holding the gun, but he quickly pulled it out of my reach as Nate came charging at us like a bull. With his head down, he tackled Todd, head-butting him in the stomach as we all got pushed into the side of the house.

The stucco scratched at my arm for a brief second before I felt Todd push Nate off and throw his body to the side, knocking me into the wall again. I wrapped my legs tighter around his body as I yanked on his hair, inflicting as much pain as I could as he kicked Nate hard in the ribs.

My heart raced as I reached forward for the gun again, only to have Todd shove me against the wall again. My back hurt from the impact, but when I saw him lifting the gun at Nate again, I knew I had to stop him. Todd might be blood, but Nate was like family. And no one fucked with my family.

Nate looked up and locked eyes with me for a brief second. I could tell he was about to charge Todd again but stopped when he realized I had another plan. I took a deep breath and then used everything I had to life myself up enough to drive my elbow into Todd's shoulder with enough force that he cried out and flung me off his back, dropping the gun in the process.

"You stupid fucking bitch," he growled, diving forward for it, but Nate tackled him first, knocking him to the ground.

I sat to the side, out of the way, as I clutched my arm against my body, trying to ignore the pain that was radiating through me from coming down on the doorknob. I heard Nate curse several times and turned my head to avoid watching the blood bath happening on the other side of me as they fought each other.

A few seconds later, I heard the sound of sirens, knowing help was on the way. Nate must have called them on his way over, though I had no idea how he even knew I was there.

The seconds felt like minutes as I waited for the police, then the heavenly sound of heavy footsteps came charging up the sidewalk as loud voices yelled around me, bodies spreading out thickly to secure the scene. Nate immediately got off of Todd and stepped back, pointing to the gun and allowing the cops to do their job. It was nice living in a small town where the local law enforcement didn't have to question who the real bad guy was.

"Hey, are you okay?" Nate asked, rushing over and bending down beside me as he quickly checked for injuries.

I sat up and shook my head, trying to make sense of it all as I held my arm.

"We need to get you checked," he noted calmly, helping me up. "I think you might have broken your arm."

"I need to call Jones and tell him what happened," I blurted out, my eyes blinking faster than my brain could process words.

"I think we should focus on taking care of you right now," he replied, swallowing hard as he looked away.

He was hiding something from me.

"What?" I asked, moving to stand in front of him so he had to look at me. "What aren't you telling me, Nate? Why can't I call my husband?"

He gently grabbed my other arm and moved me out of the way while the cops dealt with Todd.

"We'll take you to the hospital and have someone check your arm," he repeated, still not looking at me. "Let me talk with the police chief real quick and see if it's okay for you to go. They can do any questioning there."

He turned to walk off, but I grabbed his arm and yanked him back.

"Say it," I demanded, pinning him with a look. "Say whatever it is you're trying to avoid telling me." The pain in my arm continued to radiate through me, nearly unbearable as I tried to ignore it. That wasn't important right now. Whatever he was keeping from me was.

Something was wrong. Seriously wrong. Had Todd gotten to Jones before he came for me? Did something happen at work? Why wasn't he telling me anything and acting so weird?

He scrubbed a hand down his face and rubbed his lips together before looking me in the eyes.

"We responded to a fire at Lia's, and unfortunately, Jones was injured. He rushed in before we could stop him and the building wasn't secure. Part of the ceiling collapsed around him, and he was trapped under a wood beam. He's been taken into surgery, but they're unsure of how bad his injuries are. He inhaled a lot of smoke, and it took some time before they could pull him out…"

He kept talking, but I couldn't hear anything over the ringing in my ears as I fainted.

Forty-Six
Bella

"I'm fine, really," I said for what felt like the hundredth time as someone tried to check on me. After the adrenaline wore off, I realized how *not fine* I really was not knowing if Jones was going to be okay. I'd gotten to the hospital over two hours ago with Nate and had already seen a doctor to confirm my arm was broken. They had wrapped it and gave me some pain meds, but that was the least of my concerns. There still wasn't any news about Jones as the surgery was taking longer than they expected. Lia couldn't tell us much other than there were complications, and they were trying to stabilize him.

Kensy was already at the hospital when I got there, sitting in a room filled with worried firefighters concerned their brother wouldn't make it. I tried to sit with her, but it was impossible to stay still, so I chose a corner in the small room and paced back and forth until we had an update.

Finally, a doctor came out with a clipboard and a worn-out expression etched deep on his face.

"Family of Matthew Jones?" he asked, looking around the packed room.

I rushed over, feeling Kensy by my side as she held my hand and Capshaw stood on the other side. Both supporting me in ways I didn't know I needed.

"I'm his wife," I said, feeling the words catch in my throat. "I'm Bella Sanchez, soon to be Jones, but we just got married on Saturday, and I haven't had time to change my license." I reached for my purse to pull out my ID, but he lifted his hand to stop me.

"That's fine. You don't need to prove it."

"Okay," I whispered, rubbing my lips together anxiously as I waited for an update on my husband.

"He suffered multiple injuries and underwent surgery to repair as much damage as we could, as well as stop the internal bleeding. He's stable right now but has a long recovery ahead of him. We'll keep him for several days to monitor him, possibly longer if needed."

"But he's okay?" I asked, desperation heavy in my voice as it cracked.

The doctor nodded and offered a sympathetic smile.

"He's fortunate to be alive. A nurse will come out shortly and let you know when you can see him. I'll check in later to see how he's doing."

"Thank you, Doctor," Capshaw said, shaking his hand as sighs of relief echoed around us.

I let my shoulders fall, some of the tension and worry about Jones finally dissipating now that I knew he was okay. It didn't matter how long his recovery was as long as he was still there with me.

<u>Forty-Seven</u>

Jones

"You need to eat," a female voice said quietly with a stern tone.

"I'm fine. Stop trying to mother me," Bella said, equally as aggressive.

"I wouldn't have to if you would stop and take care of yourself. You're not doing him any favors by not taking care of yourself."

"Yeah, and he's in here because of me. The last thing I'm going to do is leave and have him wake up alone. I'll eat later. For now, I'm staying put."

"You need to eat, Bella," I answered, my eyes slowly fluttering open as I tried to figure out where I was and why my body felt so stiff and sore.

"Jones!" She gasped and spun to look at me, her chair sitting right beside my bed.

I quickly glanced around, noticing the hospital room we were in and Lia standing at the foot of my bed wearing scrubs.

"How are you feeling?" Lia asked, walking over and checking the monitors I was hooked up to.

"I'm fine. But please bring Bella some food."

"We'll take care of that in a minute," Lia said at the same time Bella blurted out, "I'm fine!"

"Are you in any pain?" Lia asked, writing something down on a small scrap of paper she pulled out of the pocket of her scrubs.

"Not much," I lied.

Her eyes narrowed as she studied me, looking for the answer she wanted.

"Okay, fine. It hurts like a mother fucker."

"I'll check with Doctor Dickhea—*Dickson* to see if you can have more pain meds. We've been waiting for you to wake up before we gave more."

"Thanks. But really, my biggest concern is Bella," I said, turning to look at my wife. I was relieved to see she was okay until my eyes landed on the sling her arm was wrapped in. My brow furrowed as I tried to sit up and reach her.

"What happened?" I demanded, fighting off Lia's hands as she tried to make me sit back.

"I'm fine, I promise," she assured, looking from me to Lia with an expression I didn't like. She was hiding something from me.

"What's going on? How did you break your arm, Bella?"

"I think we should focus on you right now," she said softly, reaching for my hand that didn't have a million things taped to it.

"No." I shook my head. "Tell me what happened before I find out from someone else. How did you get hurt? Was that from the fire? Did you get hurt because I couldn't get to you?"

A million thoughts flooded my mind as I remembered the fire and being outside her door, trying to get to her before I got knocked out.

"I wasn't there," she rushed out quickly, leaning forward to be closer to me. "I wasn't in the house when the fire happened, Jones. I went back to your place to get my iPad and it happened while I was gone. No one was in the house, and thankfully, the neighbors on the other side of the duplex weren't home at the time either."

"Oh, thank God," I breathed out, letting my head fall back against the pillow. "I tried calling you over and over. I was so worried something bad happened to you before I could get there. It was the worst feeling not knowing if you were okay. I thought I was too late."

"I'm so sorry." She lowered her head and started crying. I tried to lean over to comfort her but was stuck in the bed. "Come here, baby. I can't reach you, so you're going to need to come to me."

"I don't recomm—" Lia started but then stopped and lifted her hands when she saw the icy look I was giving her. "I'll be back to check on you soon."

She turned and walked out of the room while I waited for Bella to come to me.

"Please, baby. Come sit with me. Let me hold you and feel that you're okay."

She sniffled and grabbed a tissue before gently climbing into bed beside me. I made sure not to touch her arm while she watched out for any tubes or wires attached to me.

"What happened to your arm?" I asked again, more gently this time.

"Long story short, I left my iPad at your place, so I ran back to get it but forgot my phone at Lia's. When I got to your house, Todd was already inside. Apparently, he had been asking about me around town and told people he was my cousin, so they told him where you lived. He pulled a gun on me and then Nate showed up and startled us. When Todd turned around, I jumped on his back to try to get the gun out of his hand and got thrown to the ground. I'm fine, I just landed on it wrong. The police showed up a few seconds later and arrested him."

"Shit. That's—" I stopped, unable to figure out the right words.

"Insane?" she offered, looking up at me.

"To say the least. I'm so sorry you're hurt."

"No, Jones. I'm the one who's sorry. Because of me, you rushed into a burning building and almost died."

"It's kinda my job, you know," I teased, tugging her closer to me.

"Not like that, it's not. If it wasn't me you thought was inside, you would have stopped and followed command. But you didn't. You rushed in to save me, and while I love you for that, I hate that I almost cost you your life."

"Nothing can keep me from you, Bella. You are my life. Without you, there's no reason for me to live."

"And I can't live without you," she cried, tucking her head against my chest as the tears fell down her cheeks.

275

<u>Forty-Eight</u>

Bella

Three Weeks Later

"Have you gotten any new emails?" Kensy asked as we tried to talk over the loud crowd at Tipsy Taquito.

"At least five a week," I said with a frustrated sigh. "Which rules out Todd being the one to send them since he's been in jail this entire time. And every time I block them, a new one pops up. I don't know if it's the same person and they're just obsessed, or if I've somehow managed to attract hundreds of creepy people at once."

"Have you noticed anyone around town looking at you weirdly?" Lia questioned, enjoying her one free girls' night out, even though it technically wasn't a girl's night with Jones and Capshaw hanging out at a table across the room. But we'd been through enough already, so I didn't mind the extra security. Time with Lia was still hard to come by, even though she was still technically living with me and Jones until she could find something. Between the fire destroying the duplex and her long hours at work, she had more stress on her plate than anyone should have to handle.

"Umm, everyone?" I joked. "After the news spread about my cousin coming to town to kill me, no one has looked at me the same. If it's not my dirty pictures getting their attention, it's my family drama."

"I'm sorry," Kensy said, smiling softly. "I have some good news to cheer you up though."

"I would *love* some good news," I replied, setting my fork down to give her my full attention.

"Are you pregnant?!" Lia asked excitedly.

"Umm. No." Kensy shook her head and then looked across the room, smiling at Capshaw before telling us. "We've set a date for the wedding!"

"You have? That's awesome! When is it?"

"Next June. But the best part?"

I leaned forward, sitting on pins and needles as I waited. But before Kensy could speak, a woman I didn't know very well approached our table, face red as she slammed a phone down.

"Are you Bella Sanchez?" she demanded, locking eyes with me.

I pulled back, caught completely off guard by her.

"Yes," I said slowly, shaking my head when I noticed the guys getting up. I didn't need them coming over, guns blazing, until I knew who she was and what she wanted. "Do I know you?"

"No. But apparently, my son has *quite the obsession* with you."

Standing behind her with his head lowered stood a man I quickly recognized. I leaned forward, trying to see his face, but the way my skin prickled, I already knew.

"You're the guy who's been following me around town," I whispered loudly, shocked to finally see him again. Every time we thought we had him, he slipped into the darkness, disappearing into thin air.

"You've been following her?" his mother snapped, reaching around and grabbing his arm and yanking him so he stood in front of us. She was terrifying, and even though he wasn't a young kid, he still seemed as afraid of her as I was.

"Speak up when I'm talking to you," she demanded through gritted teeth.

"Yes, ma'am," he murmured, still looking down at the floor.

"Nope. You do not look at the floor while speaking. You look her in the eye and explain yourself. You were raised in God's house, and I will not have you runnin' around, acting like a hellion. Look her in the eyes and explain yourself. Right now."

"I'm sorry," he mumbled, looking up at me.

The same green eyes that had been bothering me for over a month now looked at me, but this time, they didn't spread fear throughout me as they did before. It was different. He wasn't as old as I thought, maybe early twenties, if that. Not much older than I was.

"For what, Edward? What are you apologizing for?" She looked at me and shook her head. "I swear, sometimes I wonder if he was raised in a barn. He can be smart as a whip but loses his mind when a pretty girl is involved."

I bit down on my tongue to keep from laughing. I kinda liked his mom, and from the looks of it, she was going to put him in his place.

"I'm sorry for following you around and freaking you out," he replied quietly.

Gone was the intimidating, creepy guy who had surprised me in this restaurant not that long ago. In his place was a timid kid who didn't look like they could be menacing if they tried—though I knew how he had acted when his mother wasn't around.

"Louder." His mother smacked the back of his head. "You know how to talk to a woman, so act like it."

"I'm sorry for following you around town," he said louder, practically yelling as everyone turned to look at us.

"And?" she pushed, nudging him with her arm.

"I'm sorry for scaring you and sending the emails."

"Which ones?" I asked, tilting my head.

"All of them."

"Did you keep making new email addresses every time I blocked you?"

He nodded, only to be smacked in the back of the head again.

"Boy, we're gonna have a come-to-Jesus meeting when you get home. I didn't raise you to act like this." She glared at him before turning to me. "I swear, they turn eighteen, and all common sense and logic falls out of their head. I'm sorry my son has been such a pain in the ass and caused you so much stress. I guarantee you it won't happen again. I didn't know any of this was going on until I caught him— well, we won't say what he was doing to pictures of you. When I confiscated his phone, I was disturbed by what I found, and rightfully so."

"Thank you, I appreciate it," I said, trying not to laugh as she grabbed the phone from the table and shoved it at him before pinching his ear and dragging him away.

"Well, I guess that solves that," Lia said, leaning back as she popped a chip into her mouth.

"Yeah, but there's still one big problem that we haven't solved yet," I replied, looking over at Kensy. "What's the best part?"

"We're getting married in Hawaii!"

We all squealed and shrieked with excitement as I looked over and found the guys watching us with huge smiles on their faces. Maybe things were going to be alright after all.

Epilogue
Bella
Nine Months Later

I walked through *our house*, my fingers lightly tracing over the framed photos on the wall in the hallway as I headed to the guest bedroom that was currently being turned into a nursery. After we finally went to Italy in December so I could gather the things my grandma left, we took a slight detour and spent two weeks exploring while enjoying our honeymoon.

It turned out that my grandma had very little in Italy and had left the majority of her things in Beaumont Creek. Once the terms of the trust had been met, Bart handed over the key to the storage unit where she had put everything to keep Todd from getting to it. He was still serving time for attempted murder, but I didn't trust that I would ever see the last of him. For a while, we were suspicious that he might have somehow started the fire, but it turned out it was the damaged extension cord Lia had forgotten to replace.

I was also given the key to her safety deposit box, where I found the deed to the house as well as other stuff I would have considered silly before I began this adventure, like letters I had sent to her when I was a little girl and pictures of me from different modeling agencies. I expected her to toss them like my parents did, but she kept them proudly organized with her most important documents as if they were a treasure. *I was a treasure.*

Once we got back from Italy, we decided to check on her house—the one I spent a lot of my childhood in and made the decision to move into it. Not only was it comforting to be back where she and my grandpa used to be, but it also felt like home. Jones realized he wasn't going to get rid of Lia quickly, so his house was being rented out to her until she found something else—but she wasn't highly motivated to start looking.

While sorting through her stuff in the house, I found things that sent me straight back to my childhood, as well as things that made me question everything I thought I ever knew about her.

For example, I sent her the Beaumont Creek Fire Department calendar, hoping she would get a giggle out of it. Instead, she'd circled the picture of Jones, put a heart around his head, and wrote *"this is the one"* in all capital letters. How she ever predicted that I would end up with Jones, I would never know. It was like she had known it all along and had expected something would happen between us before my birthday. I wished she was still here so I could ask her about it, but for now, I took comfort in knowing she was always guiding me.

"How's it going?" I asked, leaning against the doorframe as I watched my husband sit on the floor, putting together the crib he decided we needed to build ASAP.

"Good, I think I've finally figured it out."

"You know we don't have to do this right away. We have six months until she gets here."

He stood up and tossed his screwdriver to the floor, wiping his hands on his jeans.

"I want to be ready before she gets here so I can enjoy our time together with her."

"I know, but we have a lot of time," I assured him.

He brushed his hands across my belly, loving that I was finally starting to show. It hadn't been expected, but I couldn't stop laughing when the doctor confirmed my due date was my grandma's birthday. When we found out a few days ago that it was a girl, I laughed even harder. She had predicted in her video to me that she would be looking down on me, holding my sweet girl on her birthday.

In order to claim it, you must be married by your twenty-fifth birthday. In addition, you cannot annul or terminate the marriage for at least six months. While I would love to add that you must produce a great-grandchild as well, I won't do that since I won't be here to see it. But don't worry, I'll be smiling and looking down from heaven as you hold your sweet little girl in your arms on my birthday.

"I still can't believe we're having a girl," he said, lowering his lips to mine. "I know it's not possible, but I would love nothing more than to knock you up again once you've had this one."

"Jones!" I laughed and swatted his arm as he hugged me tighter.

"What? I love your body to begin with, but your pregnant body has me fucking harder than ever. I love how your tits and ass have already grown, but this bump—I can't get enough of it. I want to keep you pregnant forever."

"Let's start with one and see how it goes from there," I teased, though I wouldn't be opposed to having a hundred of his babies.

After I found out I was pregnant, I wrapped up my contract with Dark Vibes and explained I would be putting my career on hold indefinitely. My grandma had more money in her savings than I could ever spend in a lifetime, which meant I didn't have to work if I didn't want to.

While I missed modeling, I didn't feel the same need to do it as I had before.

Falling in love with Jones had taught me that unconditional love was greater than anything I could have ever asked for. I didn't have to be anyone I didn't want to be, and I no longer worried about what I ate, nor was I killing myself, trying to be what I thought everyone expected me to be.

He set me free in more ways than I could ever count. He showed me how to go for what I wanted, and in return, I showed him what true love felt like. Together, we worked past the demons that used to haunt us and set forth on a new forever. *Our* forever.

****

Are you ready for Lia's story? You can grab the final book in the Beaumont Creek series here https://books2read.com/u/4XwKwa

Looking for another small-town series to dive into but want more suspense? Be sure to check out my Haven Brook series! 'Til Death Do Us Part (Haven Brook Book 1) https://books2read.com/u/m2RJNR

If you're on social media, come hang out in my reader group! That's where I'm most active, and I love to chat with my readers! Facebook Reader Group:

https://www.facebook.com/groups/2945710968775398/

Other Books By Samantha Baca

The Haven Brook Series
(small-town romantic suspense):

'Til Death Do Us Part (Haven Brook Book 1)

https://books2read.com/u/m2RJNR

The Cradle Will Fall (Haven Brook Book 2)

https://books2read.com/u/b6O0QE

The Ties That Bind (Haven Brook Book 3)

https://books2read.com/u/mqgoz8

A Very Haven Christmas (Haven Brook Book 4- Novella)

https://books2read.com/u/mvqGjj

Three Strikes, You're Gone (Haven Brook Book 5)

https://books2read.com/u/mvqL2z

<u>The Dark Shadows Trilogy</u>
<u>(romantic suspense)</u>

Five Steps Ahead (Dark Shadows Book 1)

https://books2read.com/u/38Q0gO

Ten Seconds Too Late (Dark Shadows Book 2)

https://books2read.com/u/3JRgVB

Against The Clock (Dark Shadows Book 3)

https://books2read.com/u/m2YwoR

<u>The Stone Creek Series</u>
<u>(small-town- novellas)</u>

Chocolate Covered Mistletoe (Stone Creek Book 1)

https://books2read.com/u/3LRk9N

Candy Coated Promises (Stone Creek Book 2)

https://books2read.com/u/mldP5Y

Pumpkin Spiced Possibilities (Stone Creek Book 3)

https://books2read.com/u/bojdwV

<u>Beaumont Creek Series</u>
<u>(small town)</u>

Just One Time (Beaumont Creek Book 1)

https://books2read.com/u/3G52zK

Second Chances (Beaumont Creek Book 2)

https://books2read.com/u/4Aj6Z0

Third Time's The Charm (Beaumont Creek Book 3)

https://books2read.com/u/b5lEyG

Four-ever Single (Beaumont Creek Book 4)

https://books2read.com/u/4j5jMX

Fifth Wheel (Beaumont Creek Book 5)

https://books2read.com/u/4XwKwa

<u>Whiskey Mountain Series</u>
<u>(small-town- novellas)</u>

Something To Talk About

https://books2read.com/u/4X62ag

Something To Think About

https://books2read.com/u/3GWAan

Something To Believe In

https://books2read.com/u/3yVzgB

Something To Live For

https://books2read.com/u/mllEOP

<u>Sugarplum Falls Series</u>
<u>(Holiday Novellas- can be read as standalone)</u>

Blame It On The Mistletoe

https://books2read.com/u/bw1rqe

Blame It On The Eggnog

https://books2read.com/u/38PPY6

Four-ever Single

Blame It On The Candy Canes

https://books2read.com/u/31DNo7

Blame It On The Blizzard

https://books2read.com/u/b6z6XE

Standalone Books

One Last Wish

https://books2read.com/u/mqg7D9

Finding Love In Apartment 2C (novella)

https://books2read.com/u/bze9aZ

Cocky Counsel: A Hero Club Novel

https://books2read.com/u/31Kzkn

All Is Fair In Food And War (novella)

https://books2read.com/u/bp8qjX

<u>Holiday Books (novellas)</u>

Snow Place To Go

https://books2read.com/u/4A560N

A Christmas Wish

https://books2read.com/u/4EKXpE

Holiday Hijinks

https://books2read.com/u/4DP6Ze

Acknowledgments

This is the 30th book I've published since my debut novel in April of 2020, and no matter how many books I have out, I will NEVER stop thanking readers like you for choosing one of my books when deciding on your next read. Thank you for allowing me the opportunity to provide an escape into a fictional world, even if only for a little while.

I've been incredibly blessed with some of the most incredible alpha and beta readers. Amanda and Claire—I would be lost without you guys. I appreciate all of the time you gave to this book and for helping me through so much with it. You two are the true rockstars in this one! Thank you so much!

Valerie, Malissa, and Jackie thank you for being so excited about this story and for helping with the feedback you always have for me! I value each of you more than you could ever know!

Rachel, thank you for jumping in and reading this for me as everything felt like it was crumbling around me! You're a true superhero!

Thank you to the ARC readers who have read and reviewed this one. Your honest feedback is not only important to me but also to your fellow readers. Thank you for giving my book a chance, and I hope you enjoyed it!

As always, I want to thank my family for their constant, ongoing support. You lift me when I need it and are always in my corner. I love you guys!

To my husband, you know you mean the world to me, and I'm so happy you haven't divorced me over all of the book work I've given you over the years. Thanks for sticking with me! I love you more than I love Jones, which says A LOT (wink, wink).

My sweet girls, you are my life, and I hope you always remember to go after what you want. I will never stop encouraging that. I love you both so much, and you make me proud every single day.

About the Author

Samantha lives in the southwest with her husband and two small children after abandoning her childhood dream of living in a cabin in Colorado when she found that she couldn't afford to live there and was deathly allergic to the woods. When she's not writing, she's usually spouting off sarcastic remarks while drinking wine out of a coffee mug to look like a functional adult while chasing down her toddlers. She enjoys spending time with her family, watching reruns of Friends, and the 24/7 flow of coffee that can be found in her veins. Be sure to follow her on social media for updates on what she's working on.

You can find her here:

Facebook: https://www.facebook.com/AuthorSamanthaBaca

Instagram: https://instagram.com/author_samantha_baca

Goodreads: http://www.goodreads.com/authorsamanthabaca

Facebook Reader Group:

https://www.facebook.com/groups/2945710968775398/

Webpage: https://authorsamanthabaca.wordpress.com

Newsletter: http://eepurl.com/g0NcSj